T0336441

The Diary of a Porn Star

by **Priscilla Wriston-Ranger**

As Told to

David Mamet

with an Afterword
by Mr. Mamet

BOMBARDIER
B O O K S

A BOMBARDIER BOOKS BOOK
An Imprint of Post Hill Press

The Diary of a Porn Star by Priscilla Wriston-Ranger:
As Told to David Mamet with an Afterword by Mr. Mamet
© 2019 by David Mamet
All Rights Reserved

ISBN: 978-1-64293-310-9
ISBN (eBook): 978-1-64293-311-6

Cover design by Cody Corcoran
Interior design and composition, Greg Johnson, Textbook Perfect

Bettie Page™ is a trademark of Bettie Page LLC. www.BettiePage.com

Post Hill Press
New York • Nashville
posthillpress.com

Published in the United States of America

To the Memory of Bettie Page
1923–2008

Contents

A Cheerful disposition is more precious than gold,
for it cannot be confiscated at the border.

—Lao Tzu

An Introduction

What would you say of a woman whose talents led her to a career, and that career into a life of travel, study, and adventure? You would likely say, as I do, she was a fortunate human being. Some like to Test themselves against Nature. They supply us with the Explorers; some to cut people open, there we have the surgeons.

We Show-Folk delight in making things up. The young child's fantasy of heroism, love, martyrdom, or fame, is acted out, in my profession, for a living.

The results, to one whose work has been primarily in film, are visible to all: received as Art or Entertainment.

There is another side to my story. It cannot be found in my body of work, nor of the works written upon it: it is that of my personal life.

"Play" and a love of play led me to Art; it has been counter-balanced in my private life by Curiosity.

My work gave me a life of travel—both to exotic film locations and as a Personal Consultant.

Art, architecture, urban Planning, and, for want of a better term, Contemporary Anthropology were all open to me, and I embraced them. I've noted here some of my adventures—may I call them excursions?—both into the human psyche, and into our communal home, The World. I've gathered many impressions, but have come to few conclusions.

Life, love, sex, self-doubt, and the struggle for meaning are the same at the Poles, and in the Jungles. I have visited them all, and thank you for the opportunity of sharing with you some of my observations on the topsy-turvy world in which we—as per our tastes—are either doomed or privileged to live. I was blessed with a low threshold for boredom and a magnificent face and form—the combination has taken me on a long, fascinating journey. I hope you enjoy my book.

"Leafy"

I was devastated when I was rejected by Annapolis. My mother had always told us "follow your Dream." So when my dream was shattered, I returned to the Maternal Bosom, asking "what do I do now?"

She thought but a short while, and said, "get a new dream."

Well, I embraced not a <u>new</u>, but an old and discarded dream—of a life and a profession, and a calling: The U.S. Forest Service.

People speak today of "bullying." I do not think, as a child, I was bullied, but I was certainly teased. For there were (I think) several years when I would come to school wearing a Smokey-The-Bear (Campaign) hat. And I was always surprised, on sharing that childhood dream, that my school-mates found it odd.

"What? Sitting all alone in a Fire Tower, in the midst of a million acres of 'trees'...?" (As I recall one said.)

But it seemed then, as it seemed on my debarment from a Naval Career, that that life would be a magnificent chance to catch up on my reading. And, in my Grammar School days I was, in fact, called "Leafy"—the name by which my family knows me to this day—though they don't know a dicotyledon from a mono-!!

One day, after what my schoolmates used to call "her dopey foray into Taxonomy," a girl I will call "Delores" brought to school a poem by A. E. Houseman (THE SHROPSHIRE LAD), in which we find a line something like, "Blown overhead, the Aspen heaves the Bottom of its silvery leaves."

And my Delores quipped that, perhaps, the Aspen wasn't the only thing showing its leafy bottom.

That I hit her is a matter of record; and the source of much remorse on my part. There was, however, a redemptive aspect to my transgression: I resolved, on the spot, to eschew violence and Embrace the Good.

Delores had felt, from early childhood, that she possessed a Vocation. Stunned by her lack of reactivity, after my assault, I began to emulate her, not only at the Church of my denomination, but at every House of Worship within walking distance. A practice for which I thank God to this day, for I attribute to it those "shapely calves" for which I attained notoriety in my film career. (C.F. "Those Legs: Between Them She's Really Got Something," Adult Film World, JULY 1998.)

On graduation I lost touch with my school chum, encountering her some years later—not quite by accident—while part of a "fact finding mission" of the U.S. Congress. The Committee had voted itself funds to investigate sanitation on the smaller islands of the Caribbean. I was chosen to accompany them as a near-constituent of one of the congressmen.

And there, one morning, after a light breakfast of locally grown coffee and melons, on the pristine beach, heaving a net from the bow of a proa, covered in tattoos and dressed only in (what proved to be) an eel-skin *cache-sex* (G-string), was my old school chum Delores.

I cannot say which of us was the more surprised; I, to find her happily embracing the life of a subsistence fisherman, or she, to discover me "minister-without-portfolio," as it were, to a great deliberative body. Later that evening over the glowing coals of her cookfire, we sat silent and happy in each other's company; replete with the traditional seaweed-cooked "Lobster Roast," and smoking two of the Congressman's Cuban H. Upmanns. (Illegal, at the time in the United States, but perfectly consumable outside our territorial waters.)

"Yeeesssss." She drawled out. "Here is our Leafy: blown hither by what unknown storms, and where will she be blown now?"

And there, in the resurrection of a schoolyard taunt, we find the story of my Professional name—its "patness" an unfortunate mar upon its verisimilitude. But I vowed, at an early age, always to tell the truth, the whole truth, and not only <u>nothing</u> but the truth, but <u>only</u> those truths which would redound to the benefit of Humankind, shunning like the plague those which might cause anger, shame, or discomfort. (E.G. "You have an ass like a lady golfer.")

Yes, the Story of How I got my Name—its absolute truth rendered nugatory by its absence of charm. (For charm may be found most anywhere, and where it is not found there is scant little to sweeten the loss.)

On the which note, I recommend to the reader two of my particular Heroines: Gypsy Rose Lee, and Bettie Page.

Gypsy, the world-renowned striptease artist, possessed such charm that Mussolini dubbed her "American Ambassadress of Good Will." Films of her act reveal a kind humor, a love of humanity, a gentle acceptance of the Human Condition, and little else. She concluded her performances still swathed sufficiently to protect her against a (mild) Chicago winter.

What Artistry. For the true art, with Pornography, I argued regularly and long with my directors and writers, the essence, I say, taking the lesson from Miss Lee, is the Delay of Gratification.

Anyone with a Bell and Howell 8mm camera can shoot:

"Ding Dong."
Housewife: "Who can that be?"
Plumber: "It's the Plumber."
Housewife: "Come in."
(Enters)
Housewife (I): Would you like a cup of tea?"
Thumpa thumpa thumpa, et cetera.

No, to turn the Adult Film into Art one must possess both artistry and courage—the courage to trust that they'll stay in their seats until "they've come all over the upholstery." (A comment curiously attributed to Orson Welles, who made us watch a three-hour epic about a Fat man who owned a Newspaper!)

"Let's move in for the Money Shot," my director would say, after exposing two feet of film. "Not yet, not yet," I'd say. "Not yet."

Because it occurred to me—as it had to Gypsy—that everybody's either got an Innie or an Outie, and what's the mystery in that?

There isn't one.

But who listens to an Actress? Nobody.

Can you imagine the heartache of having ones suggestions—film after film—rejected out of hand?

What would it have cost them to consider them?

For instance, see the script of BEEF ENCOUNTER. (Perhaps you have seen the film.)

JOHN ENTERS HOLDING A PACKAGE.

    JOHN
This just came for you.
What can it be? (pause)

    LEAFY
Let's open it.
(opens the package)
It's my new vibrator.

> JOHN
> How does it work?

Etc.

I'd stayed up most of the night before the shoot, working on my vision of the scene and what it might contain. Viz:

JOHN ENTERS HOLDING A PACKAGE.

> JOHN
> This just came for you.
> LEAFY
> What can it be?
> JOHN
> Let's open it.
> LEAFY
> (thinks)
> Yes, then we would "know," but we'd have lost the marvelous thrill of Wonder. I remember Christmas Morning, when I was a child, and my father, in his red plaid robe—so often mended—and the slippers, gnawed-on by our old dog, Bill; and the smell of hot chocolate, wafted from the kitchen, where mom, softly humming to herself...

Etc.

I'd typed three copies of the script. One for me, one for my fellow actor, and one for the director. The director waved my offering aside.

What can one say in self-comfort? Only: "It might have been."

The Vagaries of History

Gandhi was a champion bowler.

He learned (the precursor to) the game playing Skittles while in England.

I came across a rather cryptic reference to his skill in a speech to the British Mandatory Powers during the Transition. Here he referred to the difficulty of crafting a Constitution as equal to "the seven-ten split."

This, commentators explained, was an ancient Sanskrit saying, its meaning "lost in the midst of time," but I thought "perhaps not."

I hurried to the Frankfort (KY) library as I did most mornings, as into the "arms of my First Love." Indeed, it was to those arms I hurried, for my first love was reading.

I was piqued by the quote, and remembered references to Gandhi's English Incognito, (this, perhaps, coming to your attention for the first time; and I beg your indulgence for what

I feel is not actually a digression, but, perhaps, a circuitous approach to the story of my first exposures to the Principle of Non-Violence).

These principles, as has been observed (*Life Magazine*, Spring 1989, B and D: It's Everywhere!) informed much of my understanding, and work in my beloved genre of S&M.

As always, on opening the door to a new enlightenment, various instances from the Past assert their right to parenthood. I will mention the non-violence of my friend, Delores, and will now address an instance which may have bemused or confused my readers. I refer to Delores's display of the eel-skin G-string—she who, from earliest conviction, had embraced what now is known as Total Veganism.

* * *

How did I renew our acquaintance?

On quitting the Convent, and in the period she refers to as her "transition," Delores had been "working nights" in the waterfront bars of Shreveport, Louisiana.

She found herself, after a prolonged and alcoholic business arrangement, awakening, naked and bound, abandoned on the sandy beach of what proved to be a Tropic Isle.

On rising to her knees she spied a well-built bronze-colored man dressed in a pair of yellow Speedos. He, it turned out, had just purchased her from a sea captain. Eventually adopted into the Tribe, she proved invaluable not only as a fisherwoman, but as a surrogate Mother or Aunt to its frolicksome babes.

One morning, while shucking mussels, she heard a shrill cry, and looked up to see the Chief's son thrashing about in the maws of a small shark.

Delores ran into the surf, clutching her shucking knife, and pried the child free. Carrying the tyke to shore—he shaken but essentially unharmed—she was surprised to see the Clan, assembled and still, gazing on her with awe.

It seems she had fulfilled the Ancient Prophecy that a White (Blond) (and incidentally, Natural) woman would arrive from the Sea to Protect a Chief's Son from a Monster. (The shark, by the way, by no means fully-grown, measured a scant three and one half feet; but one must make allowances.)

She was touched by the homage paid, and responded that, "It was just one of those things," and "anybody would have done the same." The tribe, however, were having none of it, and, in her debt, revived an ancient, near-forgotten Religious Order, into which she was inducted as Associate Priestess of the Near Waters; a position which carried no emolument save the right to the badge of office: an eel-skin G-string. [That garment which was to become the mainstay of my costumes during my "barbed wire" period. (The appellation is not mine. I accepted it with what I certainly hope was a modicum of "good humor;" but always felt it revealed a misunderstanding of the tone, and, more importantly, the implications of this work.)]

* * *

Gandhi's Incognito was referred to by generations of scholars as his *"wanderjahre;"* but I felt the term's acceptance (like that of the term "barbed wire") missed the period's essential nature. That year was not an interregnum between the duties of College and those of the wider world; neither, as some have suggested, a "leap in the dark" rejection of the West, and its practices of Empire. Nor was it a "bottoming-out," from which time of confusion he might begin his Climb toward Enlightenment.

No, it was, and this I found by accident, again, in that Kentucky Public Library, the beginning of a life-long love affair. Neither with India, nor Politics, nor non-violence, but with one Sara Willgood, daughter of a Burton-On-Trent draper.

And there it was. On the open shelves, a Reminiscence, mis-filed under Crafts and Textiles—the autobiography of one John Robertson, a Scot, who worked, at the Turn-of-the-Century, for Miller & Fross, Textiles—Birmingham.

Robertson served with distinction in the Royal Navy in the First World War; and afterwards, married one Mildred Fross, the Daughter of the House, and, on coming into her inheritance, moved with her to Nice where he became well-known in Yachting Circles.

In any case, there, in the autobiography, in a chapter upon "Early Years," was reproduced a sepia group photograph. The group is posed beneath the shop sign,

Willgood's-Textiles-Burton-On-Trent. And was composed, left to right, as per the description, Robertson, Willgood, Mrs. Willgood, Miss Sara Willgood, and, farthest on the right, a slight, young, dark-skinned man in a tweed suit, identified as George William Borthy. But it is Mahatma Gandhi.

My investigations took me, first, to the more extensive research facilities of the Chicago Public Library. There I found in each of the five readable biographies of Gandhi, mentions of "the Lost Year," the *"wanderjahre,"* "The Quest," and, (honestly, at least), "The Open Question." I discerned, that is, not only total ignorance but absence of interest in an exploration of that period.

Here it was that History, which had always seemed to me (though potentially informative) the least provocative of studies, revealed itself as an Aladdin's Treasure Cave, awaiting but the "open sesame" of the Possessor of a Naïve Passion. (Yes, you may have read that phrase before. I will not use this space to debate primogeniture.)

In any case, there I was, having been Summoned by a Mystery. It only remained, I jejuenely thought, to hie myself to Burton-On-Trent to lay the whole thing wide, wide open.

I was young, and had my wits about me, and was not afraid to work. And work I did, progressing first to Milwaukee, where I earned the beginning of my fares in the (now demolished) Hut-Naw-Po-Kan Hotel, and then, by Lake Steamer to Erie, then by land to Baltimore, and across by the Liner *Conte de Asuturia*, as the guest of a returning businessman.

The bracelet which he gave me—in and out of pawn these many years—rests, and I hope will rest, "for the duration," on my left wrist. The engraving on the clasp is worn almost to illegibility, but I have never had it renewed (I would think it sacrilege). It reads Q.B.S.P.

I for years supposed these initials were of a previous possessor—and I thought no less of my employer for it. After all, it's the thought that counts; but once, impoverished in Lima, Peru, a pawnbroker explained that they are Spanish for "who Kisses Your Feet"—which is a true (if partial) description of the fellow's activities during the Crossing.

Several of the Gandhi biographies, as mentioned before, refer to the Lost Year as "hitting bottom." One suggests that he had been thusly reduced by a caning he suffered in Oxford High Street. There, one day, a lengthy Rolls Royce stopped at the curb, and the footman jumped out, opening an umbrella to shield his passenger (from what all observers comment was "a very light rain indeed").

In any case, among the onlookers was Gandhi (who always loved cars). He caught the eye of the Footman and smiled his approval, the Footman responded by beating him about the head with the half-opened umbrella, while screaming, "GET BACK YOU #&*$ SON OF A &^%#."

A horrible story, made more horrible still for being a complete invention of that fantasist/plagiarist whose name I will not deign to print, but which—let those who suspect guess and they will not be far wrong—I adopted as my character name in HITTING BOTTOM (fr: *Fessez mes Joues*).

And so I went to Burton-On-Trent, and discovered, in the town archives, and in the rent-rolls, the one-year history of George William Borthy; and, in the sacristy of St. Swithins Merreydale (Burton), the marriage of George Borthy, Student, and Sara Willgood "of this Parish," and the birth of a male child some months (the 8 inexpertly but lovingly changed to a 9) later. No further record exists. There is no more mention of the Borthy, nor of the Willgood Family. The Drapery vanished in the blitz, the Churchyard offers no clue.

What is the end of the tale? Perhaps a certain sad, wistful expression on the face of a man clad in a sheet and diaper, who freed India from the British Rule.

A Tractor

Of course dogs feel shame. Anyone who'd tell you otherwise has never had a dog. Or else he had something to sell.

My mother taught me "don't trust <u>anyone</u>." Of course she meant that one could trust the people one <u>trusts</u>; but that, as I understood it, one should be careful who those people <u>were</u>. And limit their number.

For example, I once knew a very wealthy man who said, on what he might have thought was a "first date," though, to my mind, we were just having a cup of coffee, that his hobby was "doing dentistry on dogs."

I saw from his face that it was a joke, and I was expected to laugh. he was, one might say, "just making conversation," and to his mind, he, using the time, as we all do every moment, to what he thought was his benefit, was trying to impress upon me what he thought was his self-image.

Why did he think so? Because it served his purposes. OR HE THOUGHT IT DID.

Here he was, a very rich man, who'd inherited a canning factory, and run it, with the aid of inventive and lucky managers, into a worldwide concern. He took his money and retired to travel, and sports, and various wives, mistresses, and occasional help.

And being a "first date," or, at least, a first encounter, he was using that which we malign as "chitchat" to negotiate the ground rules.

So, in making a disreputable joke, he was, like many another man who might use "filthy smut," or double entendres, testing the waters, and, <u>like</u> dogs, establishing dominance. I mean it. Put two dogs, previously unacquainted, into the yard, and watch them work out who gets to do what to who.

We're no different.

How do you think he would have taken it, if I'd said "ha ha," at his joke? I'm sure that he would have counted it a victory for His Side, and who knows where it might have led?

Which, also, thanks to my mom, I did not let pass, as she always taught me to weigh <u>every</u> word spoken to me, and especially, those at a first meeting.

Who has not heard of the young boy (or girl), approached by a "non-threatening stranger," asked a question, or offered a remark, which led to this or that, and they wound up dead and mutilated in the trunk of a car, or cemented into the basement of a building?

For, think about it, where do these serial killers and rapists find their victims? On the street, my friends, or in cafes, or trolling online through the various dating services, which are little more than help wanted ads. "Help Wanted: Victim."

I was contacted on three occasions by the F.B.I., for an expert opinion on various "personals" ads. My expertise was as that of a translator, for which I felt, (and was complimented that they seemed to share the feeling), well-qualified. For was I not, in my various careers, translating hidden, clothed, masked human needs into the more healthy forms? I was.

And, in my work (unpaid, though I was offered a stipend. But how could I take money for that which any right-thinking Citizen would offer as a community service), I did the opposite: taking the reconfigured unhealthy urges of the Human Spirit and rendering them in the Original Tongue.

"Lovely, leggy Blonde, seeks middle-aged man for hazy autumn afternoons of talk, good wine and food, and more...?" (Translation: Will trade sex for dough.)

I ask you. Who, at a First Date, is going to unload the truth of their rotten, abusive (or self-abusive), neurotic, twisted self on you?

Why go on the date?

Further, and this is what I told Mother Ignatius, when she called me during her "*crise de foi*," but that's another story, why look for commitment in a bar? No, go to the Church or Service Organization. I told many many young girls, disappointed in Love, heartbroken by the unfailing repetition of their monstrously bad choices: Join the Salvation Army.

Distribute clothes to hurricane survivors, that's where you're likely to meet the man of your dreams.

I recall one person...let me pause here, I was about to say "let's call her 'Jane,' and it occurred to me that every time I've read this disclaimer it made me throw up. If her name is Jane, and you don't want to betray a confidence, call her Sue, for the love of God. And be done with it. Why call her "Jane," with the disclaimer, other than to call attention to highlight your ability to keep a secret. I'd bet that writing "let's call her 'Jane,' as likely betrays an inability to keep a secret. Because, as the French say, *qui s'excuse, s'accuse*, which is close enough to English to need no translation.

In any case, "Jane," hearing my advice to go among the victims of a hurricane, in search of a man, found that admirable, as, she said, covered in mud, cold and hungry, wet, splashed with sewage, unkempt and so on, she would "have to look into his soul," as she would be debarred from recourse to the customary recognition symbols.

That brought me up short, and, in answer to my queries, it turned out that Jane understood me to mean that she should seek a mate, not from the helpers during, but from the victims of a hurricane.

I started to laugh. And then thought "why not?" Was she not at least as perceptive as I? "And," she added, while I weighed her remark, "some of them may have been the victims of an alligator."

And, of course, they might, further testing "Jane's" resolve to take a fellow on the merits, EVEN IF, in addition to the aforementioned dishevelment, he had lost an ear, or an arm.

* * *

Well, the F.B.I. put me to the test.

They were stumped (I cannot mention the case, as it is still under adjudication, but will note it concerned several ritual mutilation-dismemberment-murders, where the victims were, on conclusion of the unspeakable rites, left sitting in a tractor.)

* * *

"...long afternoons fading into twilight and the colors of that Most Majestic Painter: at our elbow, smoky amber liquid, its taste inviting us to join the so-dear display." This was, as I will show, written by a man who'd had a tractor. Knowing the Tractor, it was softball to recognize the Amber as an unconscious echo of "Amber Waves of Grain." ("America the Beautiful"—lyrics by Katherine Lee Bates).

Someone, then, engaged in the cultivation of Wheat. But further they could not go, until I shared with them, the first (or second) "dirty joke" a boy learns on the farm.

"Q. What did the Female Tractor say to her husband?"

"...what?"

"Not tonight, John Deere."

And there it was: an UNCONSCIOUS CONFESSION. It was the cry of a farmer deprived, like the Tractor in the joke, of sex.

But this man, <u>unlike</u> (as far as we know) the Tractor, had remonstrated. And rather than, "asking again nicely," he had broken out in a homicidal rage.

The machines to which the victims had been stuffed were of various makes (predominantly KUBOTA, a Japanese Brand, which the F.B.I. had discarded as a clue because the crimes occurred in (DELETED) California, which boasts the largest dealership West of Kyoto for the KUBOTA brand.

What have we then?

A man, then, of a "Certain Age." [For who under the age of fifty? Sixty? would have heard the Tractor joke? (Noting, after all, that most of the American Population has left the farm long ago.)]

No, a man born, at mid-century, from a Rural Environment, IN THE WHEAT BELT, who liked (as per the Personal's ad) Smoky Scotch.

The puzzle began to declare its nature. And once it began, it resolved fairly quickly.

Where were the wheat-raising areas, in the 1950's, in which the John Deere (as opposed, to the FORD, and FORDSON) tractor franchises held sway? Which of those towns harbored a Youthful Offender, in, what would have been his adolescent years (say, 1960–1967), who would have had, in <u>those</u> years (and here is where I earned the admiration, if I may say, of the Government forensicists), exposure to SINGLE MALT SCOTCH? Not that he drank it, I told them, although he might have, but far, far more likely, as it was not imported in any quantity until the 1990's, and, then at a price most probably beyond the means of a wheat farmer, but that he'd <u>heard</u> of it in the tales of ex-soldiers, returning from the European Theatre. His father would have been of an age to have, almost surely, served in World War II.

The Veteran's administration supplied the identities of these servicemen, enlisted from the Wheat Belt, who had been stationed in Scotland, and a comparison of this list with that of the Youthful Offenders (as above) reduced the search to but three suspects, one of whom, traced to the area around (REDACTED), indeed proved to be the man.

A man who, in adolescence, had set fire to cats.

Horrible. Horrible. And no less horrible, to me, was the attempt at "badinage" offered by the businessman about dog dentistry. For was it not "bait?" Of course it was. He, in the manner similar to the fiend, molester, rapists, and so on, who "groom" their young prey step-by-step ("Would you like a piece of candy," etc.), was offering <u>me</u> the "bait" of transgressive comment ("joke") to see if I would accept.

Had I done so, I cannot tell what would then have been my fate.

The Lock On the Diary

One might object that this book is not, technically, a diary. Indeed, I've checked the definition, and he of the objection would be right.

Why "diary," then?

I like the word. And I think you may, too.

Especially if you are a woman "of a certain age"—old enough to recall the small, lockable notebook which was the young girl's first, precious assertion of Independence.

That lockable diary. What could it contain? What <u>did</u> it contain? For what actual secrets could the eight-or-nine-or-ten-year-old possibly possess?

The happy child, none; the mistreated, warped, or stunted, it could be the thought, "I want to kill my parents."

But why, in that case, confide it to a book?

You might say "better out than in." But it requires some wisdom or maturity to practice (or, indeed, to grasp) the relief of confession.

But it is this relief and practice I embraced, during the first, early years of my professional life. And those regimes of yoga, meditation, past-lives therapy, and prayer which, increasingly, fill my day, are an attempt, perhaps, to prise from my soul those secrets which are "better out than in" and to examine them. For we can't fix what we can't see.

The young girl's diary might contain forced references to a (as yet fictitious) budding sexuality, meditations upon adornment, or confessions of admiration for a chum.

Mine, which you hold here, (for I am that Young Girl, though now aged) will similarly hold (and may you find it so) intimations of the existence and/or the approach of a new reality.

This New Thing, hid in the mature Female—held, IN UTERO, if you will, like the truths of Sexuality in the prepubescent—is by turns, beckoning, nagging, troubling, misunderstood, surprising, or, as transcribed, totally false.

You will not find here my day-to-day, year-to-year musings about clothes, nor whether "Johnny really likes me," nor adorable gushings about shoes, but rather ruminations about the attractive and troubling things, thoughts and feelings of a more-travelled soul; these including but not limited to, thoughts of or recollections upon sex, cannibalism, national identity, and sports.

And neither are these musing limited by date (as in the traditional understanding of a "diary"). They come to you as they come out of me, if you will, in their own form.

I know "diary" comes from the Latin meaning "day"—I was brought up speaking not one but two languages, the English of the wider world, and the Afrikaans which my parents brought with them. Which prompts the suppressed memory of my affair with that Agent of the F.B.I.

It was he who congratulated me upon my discovery of the "clue," of "Amber Waves of Grain."

We know that admissions are calculated to bring two people together. We offer them, as we offer the sacrifice of our friends ("gossip"), hoping, thus, to "cast bread upon the Waters."

* * *

We were in the secure "off-site" headquarters of the Serial Killer Task Force, sharing another cup (for me, of coffee, for him, a Mormon, Kukicha Tea), and a cherry Danish, cut in half by one swipe of his switchblade.

I admired the knife, and he offered it to me as a gift. It had been taken, it seems, from the hand of a murderer-kidnapper, cornered in the topmost story of his "council flat," in Wandsworth, England, where my Agent had been "seconded" to MI5.

The building was ringed with lights and armed assault troops, but my friend was just outside the door supposedly as an "observer," but armed-and-ready, should the need arise.

The cornered malefactor was exhorted to give himself up, by an Anglican Cleric, reading to him from the Book of Common Prayer.

"I have one better than that," the criminal said, "if by chance thine eye offendeth thee, pluck it out, man, and be Whole; but be a man, stand up and End Thee, when thy sickness is thy soul."

The Cleric, and the Intelligence fellows were stumped, but the Mormon said "A. E. Housman, A SHROPSHIRE LAD, 1886."

The kidnapper heard him, and said "send <u>that</u> man in, I want to talk to him."

Well, talk they did, and after a quarter-hour, the murderer surrendered to my friend, on parting, handing him the switch-blade (which I was schooled <u>not</u> to refer to as a "Stiletto") with which he had intended, should he exhaust his "ammo," to take his own life.

[The switchblade is an "automatic" or push-button folding knife, from which the blade, held by a spring in the handle, makes the half-circle into usefulness, pivoting from the handle's side. A <u>Stiletto</u> blade emerges straight out from the handle's end; and though some might find the terms interchangeable, I was taught to use them with precision, a gift I value, if I may, as much as the knife, which now does duty as a paperweight, on the screened porch of my "summer house." (A cabin, really. I've used the term ironically for so many years that, eventually, it stuck. Perhaps you've had a similar experience.)]

In any case, <u>my</u> offering to this agent, on our first meeting, was a girlish yes, but <u>as</u> girlish, innocent confession, was that

I was confused as a child, by the opening line of the song under discussion. (AMERICA THE BEAUTIFUL, 1910)

"Oh beautiful

"For Spacious Skies

"For Amber Waves of Grain."

My home-tongue being Afrikaans (a dialect, of course, of German), I understood the preposition "for" (German *"ver"*— Afrikaans *"vor"* = "well..."). It has its cognate in the English "for"—as forbidden, forlorn, et cetera. And, in the Germanic Tongues may, confusingly, mean un- re- pre- self- et cetera, as *voertske, voertuig*: "go out/away."

I said I was always ashamed that I had accepted the word "forspacious" as, obviously, a derivative of German-Afrikaans, but I had never neither looked it up, nor asked anyone for a translation. I suppose, I said, that I was ashamed of my ignorance.

He replied that he was one of the countless Americans who had, ignorantly, pledged allegiance to the Republic for Richard Stans, without ever questioning that notable's history.

As a practicing Mormon, he said, he found his act, on mature reflection, unworthy. Why would one raised as a Man of Faith, coming from a four-generation Military Family, and destined for a life of Sworn Service to his fellow citizens, pledge allegiance to one whose nature and worth was completely unknown? Well, there you have it, I said, and we embarked on a long, long career of mutual esteem.

When his wife died he proposed to me. But I, by that time, fully committed not only to that career which was mine when we first met, but to the various "good works," which my wealth and notoriety allowed me to pursue, could not accept his offer. I, sadly, refused.

And, yes, I examined my conscience for signs of cowardice, or religious prejudice. For I had discovered, as part of my soul-searching, the phrase "damned if I'll spend the rest of my life one of a multitude of wives, washing the diapers of his great-grandchildren somewhere south and east of Salt Lake."

I know that the Mormons no longer practice polygamy (to speak of). I found my rumination shameful, and only excused myself on recognizing that my foray-into-shame was one way to distance myself from the possibility of The Other Choice. I accepted that difficult choice. It was not made because I could not embrace the Doctrines or the practices of the Latter-Day Saints (what did I know of them?) but because I a) lacked the courage; b) was not over-possessed of the ambition to begin a new life.

My religiously intolerant "Meme" was but a (disguised) expression of disgust at myself, and how could a woman so-flawed even <u>think</u> of binding her troth to such a good and upright man?

In addition to which, I had, and have no wish to move to Utah. Though I have, over the years, spent quite a bit of time there on the Slopes, for the maintenance and preservation of which I am grateful to that Beehive State.

Nine-Ball

Now here is a curious thing. I've mentioned earlier that my schoolyard "cognomen" was Leafy. That, however, was not how I received my professional name—that name under which I would achieve what fame accrued to me in that portion of my existence—that is, film.

For I account it of greater worth to have done this or that in: Bosnia, South Central Los Angeles, and with the men and women of the Jet Propulsion Labs, than to've worked, however (to my mind) well, in the entertainment industry.

The diminutive "Leafy," came to me through the linguistic environment of my childhood. For, though raised—and here let me set the record straight—in Muskegon, Michigan, my parents were first generation Afrikaans. In the home, then, I absorbed not only the language (used, to refer to those things—or rather <u>that</u> thing which, by its revelation as Taboo held for us the greatest interest and thus, an irresistible incentive to linguistic mastery), but an introduction to obfuscation.

[Young people nowadays speak, or did, when they went to college, of having "taken," French, or Spanish. This, to an even slightly polyglot (speaker of more than one language) marks them unfailing as unable to command, in the second tongue, even a cup of coffee. For one, whether in the realm of linguistic, or in the hurly-burly of acronyms, catch-phrases, and allusions on a film set, does not master the new speech by "taking it," but, of course, only by immersion. (A process which I alluded—and, yes, some have "caught it, and commented upon it, in GET IN THE POOL.)]

To return to this reminiscence, which might be titled "coincidence," if I (or you) believed in it, I was raised in Muskegon, Michigan, and came by my "British" accent legitimately. Its repercussions, in my life, are numerous indeed.

For we are animists, and see some sort of order and connection both in the connection of that day's traffic with the good-or-bad news we've received that morning, and with the workings of the World Bank. (Whatever <u>that</u> is.) Seriously, does anyone know what that is? I don't. And I once spent two and a half weeks with a man who'd received a certain Scandinavian Prize in Economics.

There is this to be said for a liaison with an elderly man: after the first "passage-at-arms," you can, at least potentially, get him talking and "learn a thing or two." And I am not sure even those folks in Quantum Physics understand the age-old term "coincidence," as other than the refusal of an arrogant mind to observe or intuit a deeper order.

(All those smaller and smaller particles whipping around, each, acknowledged every succeeding decade, with properties weirder than the ones we knew before...)

But I was raised by first-generation immigrants. Now they, as children, had of course mastered English, but their parents, my grossvater, und grossmutter, had done so only imperfectly, and they carried with them, from South Africa, the smatterings of English they had learned there in their Sporting Goods Store (which catered both to Afrikaans, and to the occasional Englander, come to examine the shops rather excellent collection of pre-war (World War II) Gulf of Tonkin (Vietnamese) split-bamboo rods—without equal in the world.

I had one with me in my Baltimore apartment many years, until the dog ate it. We never know the worth of "it's no use crying over spilt milk," until beset by rage and loss and having to choose between licking our wounds, forgetting them, or deepening them.

So the limited shop language of my grandparents' day contained the Englishism of the between-the-wars Brits— those tag-phrases so beloved of the inexpert and limited speakers of a foreign tongue.

I will cite "jolly good," "laughing like Larry" (I've tried in vain for years to find the derivation), "cheery-bye," "up the spout," and others of that time, no doubt used, even by the English Speakers in Grandfather's shop, with a certain amount of irony, but translated to Michigan, to my parents, and, thence, to me, with the force of any "family speech" or jargon.

In any case, there I was, on the set of my third film as "Gertrude, She-Vixen of the Waffen S.S." Our advisor, an elderly man, had himself been an Oberst (Major) in that Corps.

The actor—his role written and directed to portray a "similar" character, had just suffered a motor scooter accident, minor but sufficient to debar him from work that day. (His body was covered with road rash, and his skin sufficiently delicate that application of body-makeup to cover the rash would have caused medical complications. We would have had to slather the stuff over him like spackle. Or an inexpertly applied driveway sealant.)

The German Major volunteered he would be most happy to take the fellow's part, and began to disrobe.

"Pris," the director said, "would you mind playing the scene with the Nazi?"

"I'd as lief not," I replied.

Which is the true origin of my stage-name.

But recollect the coincidence, for it had been the name I was called in the schoolyard. And the two circumstances were, neither in time, nor place, nor content, in any way similar. Nor were the two words (Lief and Leaf) etymologically linked. Nothing like it.

And here's a third thing: I learned to shoot pool on the 4 ½ x 9 basement table of Mr. Rutusnik, our next-door neighbor. I had learned from his wife, Bala, to make pierogi at their house. She saw me, at about eight-years-old, peeping over the fence, obviously enthralled by the cooking odors of that ethnic food. She invited me in, and taught me not only pierogi, but blini, monkuchen (poppy seed cakes), eintopf, and many other delicacies local to her native Pomerania.

Her husband liked to shoot pool. He ran an auto repair shop and had done sufficiently well to have fitted his basement out as a "den." He had the Budweiser sign, a juke box, a bar and a pool table.

Inviting me down, one day when his wife was marketing, he had me on the table (then covered). After initiation he removed the cover to cleanse it of a spot (visible to his Germanic eye for cleanliness, but not to me. I recall saying "I don't see anything," and he replied, "My wife will."

He removed the cover, and attacked it with a series of cleaning products he kept in a nearby cupboard. Their profusion and his expertise might have revealed to a more knowing child the frequency of his basement activities.

But I was young, and the only observation which at that time occurred to me was that we must not upset the Old-World orderliness of his house, and thereby displease his wife.

He'd finished cleaning the cover (as I write I recall the rather sharp scent of pine, or pine-derivative-based cleanser). We heard the front door open, and the steps of his wife, descending the basement stairs; I found a pool cue thrust into my hands. I heard her say, "they were out of confectioner's flour," and then the clink of the pool balls, one against the other.

Mrs. Rutusnik came downstairs smiling. Her husband bent over the pool table, considering what (I later learned) was a challenging side-pocket bank shot, looked up and said, "I'm teaching Little Pris to play."

And so, to complete the ruse, I was invited, at least two and sometimes up to four times a week, to come down to the basement and learn pool (or, more correctly, "Pocket Billiards"—Pool being the copyright name of the game, patented and in possession of the Brunswick Balke-Collender Company of Chicago.)

I progressed through Straight-Pool (fourteen and one continuous pocket billiards), into Eight Ball, Nine-Ball, Rotation, no-touch, one-hand, and, thence, naturally, into the finer points of hustling.

I was competing in the 19xx Michigan Junior Women's Invitational "World of Nine-Ball" Tournament, under an assumed name. Why, you might ask, suspecting (due to the nature of my later professional life) a desire for anonymity, but you would be wrong. I played under an assumed name, as I was underage.

The "Junior" Competition was for girls 16–19, and I was eight months shy of the minimum age.

I arranged, with the help of my school's Assistant Principal, to borrow the school record of an older girl. (It was returned, no one the wiser; and though I understand, as did he, this was a minor transgression against the girl, no one was harmed. She and he eventually married.)

Prior to the tournament, I'd played the game only in the Rutusnik's Basement. The mores, language, shifts, strategies and hustles of the Pool World came to me later, and all over the world, from games in locales as diverse as a waterfront dive in Surabaya, to, yes, a Sultan's Palace in an Arab Country I will not name here.

I'd learned (and learned well) to "play safe," that is, when presented with "no shot," to leave the cue ball in a position which made it difficult for my opponent to shoot.

This position, in which the ball was intentionally left, was called a "leave." And Mr. Rutusnik and I practiced the art of the leave as an essential of the game.

Well, in the quarterfinals of the Michigan Invitational, I had no shot whatever on the object (here the two-ball). I "played safe," leaving the cue ball in a position impossible for my opponent. And she remarked "nice Lief, Erikson."

Yes, the delights of language.

Religious Freedom

Speaking of the Vagaries of Language, consider this (which I reveal, I think, here for the First Time), in SAND IN YOUR CRACK, (released in the Arab Word as VILE LEGACY OF THE CRUSADERS), the Heroine (myself, as LEAFY), is attempting to cheer her accountant out of a funk engendered by his inability to comprehend the (1985? 86?) Revisions in the Tax Laws.

She tells him a joke.

Knock knock.

Who's there?

Hyman.

Hyman, who?

Hyman the Mood for Love.

As per the script, the accountant, recognizing the intentions of Leafy (as opposed to the, granted, mediocrity of the joke), laughs and things progress apace.

But when the film was released in Arabia, the distributors demanded not only a change in the Title, but the excision of the joke. I argued long and hard that, without the joke, there was no reason (dramatically) for the Accountant to cheer up sufficiently to share with Leafy the underlying cause of his disaffection. (That he had forged his C.P.A. certificate, and was afraid of discovery, shame and financial ruin.)

Absent the device (his recognition of "Leafy's essential good-nature, and, so, of his decision to trust her not only with his secret, but with his you-know-what"), there is no reason for their decampment from the Financial Planning office into the broom closet. But the Arabs insisted on excising the joke.

Wait, I said, why not keep the joke, but overdub the (to them, objectionable) "Jewish" name.

Give it a try and we'll listen, they replied, and so I did, and the film (which had to be dubbed, anyway, into Arabic) had the joke rewritten thus:

Knock knock.

Who's there?

Mustapha.

Mustapha, who?

Mustapha half hour of your attention.

That was the gag as I'd rewritten it, and I supposed, naïvely, that that was the gag they used. But it was not. Their version ran:

Knock knock.

Who's there?

35

Mustapha.

Mustapha, <u>who</u>?

Must a fastidious Muslim have to waste his time which might otherwise be spent in prayer, luring a mere woman into the broom closet?

I was offended by the redubbing (which took place without my knowledge). I learned of it, only after the film's release, in a letter from a very personable young Saudi Engineering Student (studying at Tulane). I thought the new translation an insult, minimally to the writer (me); but, what the hell, I'm used to it, as is <u>any</u> writer, sometimes wooed, sometimes bribed, but always, finally bludgeoned by the disaffected purchaser (producer), unable to metabolize the difference between his unfulfillable desires (for the script) and the limitations of the power of dramatic writing.

No, I was used to being kicked to the curb, as writer and as performer, but I was mortified at the conjunction of my name with, and the use of my work in support of the disenfranchisement of women.

No. I did not like it.

And I spoke out, as you may know, on Belgian Television against the re-dubbing. But, I told my host, I foresee a World, and that world not too distant, when my Sisters, living under patriarchal rule, may throw off those ancient strictures and live, as Equals in the World, as God Intended us. How, the interviewer asked, could that be? In Theocracies where women were bound not only by Legal, but by Religious

Practices upon which Legal restraints were based. Would it be necessary for Woman, in order to embrace Modernity, to Abandon their religion?

No. I said. I cannot accept that eventuality. For they are entitled not only to co-equal Freedom with Men, but the Freedom (as should accrue to all peoples) to choose and practice the Faith of their Choice.

Well, how would you conjoin, for example, I was asked, the Freedom of Modernity, with the Wearing of the burkha?

After but scant thought I replied (not at all completely in jest, though it was taken that way), "What about a 'see-through' burkha?"

This is, famously, the quip which got me thrown off of Belgian Television, though I, after, believe me, <u>much</u> soul-searching, cannot charge myself with its eventual (the next week) bombing.

I have found myself, yes, at the center, and even accused (praised?) for being the prime-mover in various controversies. And some of them have gotten beyond my control.

But as I said at The Hague, "I just go where I'm sent, and do what I'm told when I get there"—a phrase I cribbed, of course, from Douglas MacArthur, during the Mexican "punitive" expedition of 1914—a, thankfully, near-forgotten episode in our Foreign Policy.

I consider myself—I would not say, "An Ambassador of Good Will," but, certainly, as a proud citizen, a representative, for good or ill, of my Country. And, when abroad, I try to recall

my position, and to act accordingly. Small minds may miscon-
strue, and unoccupied minds delight in gossiping about the
actions of the Prominent; but, in our defense, and, I suppose,
as their excuse, we're all just Human Beings.

An Orange

I do not know if more information is a good thing or not. Somebody said that nothing's either good or bad, but thinking makes it so.

I see the reasoning behind this advice. It makes the individual responsible for her feelings in a world where, as Bettie Page once said, "you can't control outcomes."

But there are certain things which <u>are</u> bad. Nazis, for example. Or, I was about to say, "a toothache," but it occurs to me the "good" of a toothache is to warn you to have your tooth looked at.

I do not like canned tomatoes, and no force on earth could force me to like them. yes, yes, yes, you might say, how about "hunger?" Touché. For "hunger," could, though but a feeling, be considered "a force on earth." And a philosopher more skilled than I might craft some sort of axiom to that effect: that nothing's either good or bad except canned tomatoes when you're hungry.

But here again, we see the operation of that principle which (as I am human) has vexed me all my life: that expanding any idea far enough will render it useless; just as contracting it sufficiently (in the words of Oswald Spengler) (my friend the Ophthalmologist, not the philosopher), can excuse any bad thing as good.

The information to which I refer is that I obtained through the Freedom of Information Act regarding my rejection at Annapolis, the United States Naval Academy. I was, as I've said before, heartbroken when they turned me down. As was the Congressman, who'd, quite graciously, nominated me. And yes, there was a certain amount of talk in Muskegon about the reasons behind his (to small minds) inexplicable championship of my Naval Career.

Yes, yes, he did "get fresh," at that first meeting. But any girl of moderate looks (and what, finally, are childbearing years?) can and might use any advantages she has to Get Ahead, and that is her business. Is this to say, young ladies, that she should "lay down" for any Tom, Dick or Harry with a carton of Camels? No, and again no. But Appearance is, good or ill, a calling card. And just as two otherwise identical applicants (for anything) offer the judge a conundrum which he will refer not to the mind but to the senses; so, equally, if you can Spruce it up, (or use it if it "IS" up), for gosh sakes take advantage.

Shame shame, some Feminists may cry. But people do inherit different traits. Or they may inherit money, or connections, and if they should not happily use them, who's the sonofabitch who'd put himself in charge of deciding?

That's what "my old Nurse" told me. Or is one of a fine appearance to shut up inside a Paper Bag? [Irrespective of whether or not SHE CHOOSES to sit on a Congressman's Lap (or, indeed the lap of any elected Representative.)]

Why was I rejected by the Naval Academy?

My grades were superb. I was the Captainess (as they called it then) of the Debating Club. ("Resolved: That the United States Should Annex the Dominican Republic.") [We went to the Regional Championships, and I, having been assigned the negative, employed my (usually definitive) "and what would we do with Haiti?" But, to my chagrin, the other girl had an answer.] I was the State Junior Women's Pocket Billiards Champion, and I put up a good front.

I sailed through the admittance tests, and the preliminary interviews, and I was invited to Annapolis (Maryland) for a final series of encounters, which, I was assured, were, essentially, formal. ["A holdover, I was told, from the Days of Sail." Ha ha, I thought, for, should the Authorities become "nostalgic," I was, coincidentally, up on the "43 Knots Every Girl Scout Must Know." Which, I am ahead of you, yes, I did put to good use in the "Tied-Beaten-Shackled and Corrected series. ("TBS and C," to its aficionados.) I could tie a three-second bowline (the trick is easy once it's demonstrated) throw the clove hitch, and the lesser hitches, and as a party trick, perform the Turk's Head, Monkey Head, or Matthew

Walker.) Several very observant viewers of TBS and C wrote commenting on the last, which disappeared from the Blue Jacket's Manual in 1885!]

I came prepared for the "Pro-Forma Interviews," dressed in a tight-but-not-too-tight suit of Barathea—in homage to The Naval Tradition—and carried, in my hand, a pair of white gloves. The Officer on duty at the Annapolis Gate checked my identity against his list, and directed me to my first meeting. I glanced down at the clipboard, and saw that it was with an office entitled "Career path." I was directed across the (beautiful) campus, and off I went.

I thought it odd to be asked to discuss a "career path," as it seemed to me that the career I was in the process of choosing was "the Navy." So I asked a rather nice looking Marine officer, and he explained that, yes, "the Navy" was the Overall Career, but, within the Organization there was, Surface, Aviation, Judge Advocate, and so on, these being, in toto, a list of occupations equal in size to that of any small town.

In I went. I found a balding man in the uniform I, through my study, identified as that of a Lieutenant Commander.

He was sitting stock still at a bare desk in a small empty office. I sat primly down. He looked at me and took, from his desk drawer, a small paper bag (about the size in which we, as kids, brought our lunch to school).

From the bag he took an orange. He placed it on the desk, and said, "Do you know what this is?"

Oh no, I thought, the poor man, sitting, at the end of a career, in a make-work job, has gone mad. He is puzzled by the identity of an orange. Not wishing to embarrass him, I kept silent.

After a while he nodded, and took from the top drawer of his desk a sheet of paper covered with an inkblot. he showed it to me and said, "What is this?"

Well, I thought, not wishing to appear a fool, "I'll play along."

"It's an inkblot." I said.

He pushed the paper further toward me.

"What do you see in it? He asked.

"Um. Ink," I said.

He shook his head, and put the paper back in the drawer.

"That'll be all," he said, and I left.

It turned out that fellow knew perfectly well what an orange was (a citrus fruit), but that he was quizzing me.

Why?

Because as I learned, twenty years later, from the Freedom of Information Act, I had been denied admittance to the Naval Academy having been deemed psychologically incompetent. For the Lieutenant Commander was not a graying end-of-the-road Guidance Counselor (we've all met them) but the Chief of Psychiatry of the institution. I had been sent to the wrong office, and he had been expecting the psycho daughter of a great industrialist, who'd been granted a "courtesy interview" as a favor to her dad.

She (you'd know her name) was <u>barking</u>; and though fabulously wealthy, was later arrested for shoplifting in an auto supplies store.

But was I happier on knowing the (completely absurd and meaningless) reason for my rejection than I'd been in wondering.

Was there a Providence in all this? I must say "Yes." For, if I'd gone into Naval Aviation (which would have been my choice), I never would have had the career with which I was blessed, nor met those people (good or bad, but generally interesting) the relationships with whom have formed the warp and woof of my life.

The Bohemian Grove

How many people can say they've been trout fishing with Shimon Peres? Well, that was an experience which shaped my life. In 19XX I was invited by a Friend to accompany him to the annual encampment of The Bohemian Grove. This 300 acre rustic retreat, some hour east of San Francisco has, for near one-hundred years, been the refuge and resort, for one week in July, to World Leaders in Government, Business, Politics, Philanthropy, and the Arts.

The Members and their guests (all men) romp around in sheets fashioned into togas, sing Campfire Songs, and plot the destiny of the world.

Women are not allowed.

However. I was dining one evening at a most exclusive restaurant in Manhattan. A very dark-skinned, elegant gentleman in a dashiki came toward my table flanked by two serious-looking bodyguards. I recognized the gentleman from the cover of Time Magazine, and rose extending my hand.

He took my hand, glanced down, I thought, to kiss it, and remarked, of my bracelet, "it is this which has emboldened me to interfere upon your business conversation." Here he inclined his head in apology toward my evening's companion. "Do you know," he asked me, "the meaning of this amulet you wear?"

I didn't want to tell him I'd received it from a cloakroom attendant in Sierra Leone who'd lost my anorak.

I'd told her "forget it," but she, as I supposed, in the "pride of her profession," would have none of it. She took the amulet from her wrist and fastened it upon mine.

To the statesman I replied "no."

"I do not have the privilege to know its meaning. Would you tell it to me." He said he could do more than that, that he would demonstrate the Symbol's Power, but, for me to fully appreciate the ceremony's significances, he must relate to me its history as a Tribal Tattoo.

I told him I'd love to see such a tattoo, and he said, "come with me,' and led me to the Men's Room.

Our friendship flourished. We discussed, frequently, the cross-cultural coincidence of myth and symbol. We were, in fact, deep in a fascinating explication of the spontaneous and universal appearance of the "trickster" myth (in both East and Western Thought).

We hurried, at night, each with his or her offering of fact or deduction, to his apartment close to the U.N. Loki, Ragnar, the "Old Man Coyote" of the Sioux; yes, even the American figure of the Assistant Principal...the more we explored and shared, the greater our delight in the exploration.

We covered his kitchen table with diagrams, notes, newspaper clippings, and I-don't-know-what. And it seemed that we were, in exhausting, not the Topic, but our ability to address it while retaining any Distance. As we moved, that is, toward the "formulation of a Thesis," he was invited to Bohemian Grove. And I, being a woman, could not go.

Well, we've all had a similar experience: on the cusp of the annunciation of a previously pre-verbal understanding, on the brink of some new Wisdom, a conscious and transformative, a <u>new</u> revelation, the phone rings, and it's gone forever.

I had come to his apartment fresh from my usual afternoon in the Anthropology Stacks of the 42nd Street Library, and was bursting to share with my friend, my discovery of "Chinnotka, the Salmon Who Could Never Get Anything Right."

This was (I felt and continue to feel) an absolute correlative of (his discovery) "Ching Dao, the Shy But Effective Panda."

But, before I could speak, he said he was called to San Francisco, to the Bohemian Grove, there to discuss (informally, and, so, potentially effectively) his Country's possible transition to Nuclear Power.

I saw tears in his eyes, as he toyed with the materials I'd brought him—yes—as a gift. he placed my notes, reverently, on the Kitchen Table (our Study). And turned away.

"Take me," I said, "take me as your Guest."

"Men only," he said. (The first I had heard either of this restriction, or of The Grove itself.)

Reader, I cut my hair, borrowed a (slender) friend's British-cut suit, and went to the Bohemian Grove in drag. (And I'm sure I was not the first.)

On arrival I changed from my male costume into the locally-appropriate sheet, and no one was the wiser.

Yes, they were happily wandering the grounds, pissing on trees, and, watching me squat, may have had their suspicions, or perhaps they merely thought me shy.

That may have been it, as, around the Campfire, they took to chaffing me. E.G.: "Young Chapman-Harris—'my adopted name'—is squatting so that no one will get a peek at his dick. HA HA. Squats in the bushes like a girl. I hope there's no poison sumac there! That'd be a whole lot of explaining to do when he gets back to Johns Hopkins" (my cover tale).

On the third evening or so the men were seated around the campfire discussing the market in Rare Earth Metals and singing smutty songs. We were all full of various rare vintages of Rieslings (flown in by the heir to the second-largest fortune in pharmaceuticals in Germany), and I had to pee.

Wandering out of both the spell and the illumination of the campfire, I found myself a (I thought) sufficiently secluded knoll, hiked up my sheet, and, having found my relief, started back in the dark. My eyes, however, had not regained that night-vision ruined by the jumping flames, and I walked into what I at first, took for a tree, but discovered, when it spoke, it was in fact the Prime Minister of Israel.

"I saw your bum," he said, "and either you're a girl, or I've turned into a Homo."

Well, I didn't know how to take it, but the man laughed, and then I laughed, and I saw we'd broken the ice. He joined our group (or Lodge, as they call them there), and was a happy participant in all our discussions, quick to addend an insightful comment, or diffuse a potential dispute with what we would only recognize much later was wit.

Now and again he would offer a thought, and say "don't you think so, Chapman-Harris?" I would smile or nod in deference to his greater wisdom, understanding this however (or additionally) as an "in-joke." But the others understood these infrequent but pointed attentions toward me as a "crush" on his part.

My friend, particularly, found it maddening.

"What the hell are you doing?" he said, "Letting that ancient Kike make up to you during the Sing-a-Long?"

But what could I do about it? I couldn't tell my friend that our secret was discovered. He would (or thought he would) have been mocked by these, the great of the world, for his lack of ability to Keep his Dick in his Pants.

Now, the Traditions of the Grove, of course, encompassed the odd-instance (as does any tradition) of transgressions-of-the-norm. C.F. the sexual life of the World's Navies, squinting at what a less enlightened time called "sodomy." Such also, (latitude, in the service of Reality), was an (unspoken) aspect of the Grove, where there might pass unnoticed instances of camaraderie, which, in inebriation, passed beyond mere "horseplay." (And there were, on the site, various farm animals whose utility, I believe it was understood, extended beyond mere ornament.) And, while to discover the subvention, as it were, into the Grove of a Female might occasion in those acres mere laughter (or, indeed fame), revelation of such antics to the outside world would be (to my friend) ruinous. How serious was the risk?

And were there not among us, newsmen, that July, who, though risen, through age and a distinguished mien, from the status of mere "newspreaders" "Sit there, read this and look sad," to consideration as pundits or indeed philosophers?

Must they not, whores that they all essentially are, repeat, if not broadcast, the delightful (to the Gossipy Mind) tale of the Black Champion of Black Africa, and his dedication, to the Ancient Ways, and his (five or six) wives, such tale now sweetened by the enchantingly sordid news of his affair with a (white) pornographic actress? If such got out, its (to him) most operative component would be not shame but <u>ridicule</u>: and, see that it occurred at a Secret Conclave of (generally White) bigshots, who, though ostensibly convened to carve-up-the-goods-of-the-world, still retained time to cheat on their wives and piss on trees...

(I must say that I did not find the Company of my Lodge, on average, more generally wise than any assemblage of men randomly found at a truckstop. I do exempt my friend the President-for Life, and Shimon Peres.)

Well, I was packed off back to New York, and I'd say "no harm done," but the unfortunate sequel to my friend's umbrage at Shimon Peres was his Country's "pivot" away from an agreeable "neutrality" and toward a disposition to Iran and its abhorrence of the Jewish State. And it was this which I was asked later to address.

* * *

Back in New York, I found, under my door, a note from "a friend and an admirer," inviting me to luncheon at Grace a' l'Espagna (then, and perhaps now, the Only Michelin Five Star Restaurant West of Le Havre).

There I went, I entered the restaurant and was greeted by a well-set-up, fortyish man in acceptably cut sharkskin suit. He stood. "Ms. Wriston-Ranger," he said, "Please call me Paul." Over the shrimp cocktail he explained to me he was from the Mossad (the Israeli Secret Service) and had an invitation for me from a Mutual Friend, who, he said, "and I think this will be sufficient to identify him, once did not see you pissing on trees."

On concluding lunch he gave me an envelope containing airline tickets, five thousand dollars in cash, and a gift certificate from Paragon Sports (17th and Broadway), to which was stapled a note "buy trout fishing equipment."

A Spider

I t has been suggested that I've had an odd life.
Well, it doesn't feel odd from my side, of course.

I believe the difference is a matter of philosophy, and, after some thought, I've come to understand it <u>thus</u>: when you're buying a car, the salesman will point out, among its many features, the paint job and the interior.

Now, the paint job is of some importance, as, when you walk up to your car, you will notice it. And you may approve or accept, or, indeed, disapprove (I once had a World War II era Jeep in Lime Green) (but it ran well); but in any case, you will identify that car, which is <u>your</u> car, by color.

We're told, from early Youth, at least I was, that Beauty is Only Skin Deep. I have two comments.

I once said this to a dermatologist, who replied, "Yes, but so is skin;" and, I recall, my old Grandmother would say, "beauty is as beauty does."

But we're all suckers for a pretty face. And sometimes the possessor of this face is the biggest sucker of all. For he, or she, may spend much time (and <u>will</u> spend <u>some</u> time at least, if they are "conscious") trying to determine why they have been chosen. For a shapely form and melting eyes may get you out of a traffic ticket, just as a square chin and a winning way may obtain for you the Presidency.

Why, you might wonder, "me?" And you may vow to use your (free) gift wisely, or may resolve to exploit it for all its worth and call this exploitation "only my due." You can, (and I believe I have tried to) come to grips with an inheritance, and vowed to use it wisely.

And many times I've failed (as you've failed, too); and, having failed have warred between a renewed resolve to "behave," and an arrogant indictment of those I have slighted or (may God forbid it) wronged.

Well. That's my life. And I believe the life of a Sex Symbol is no less particular than that of a monarch, bred and trained for <u>that</u> Ceremonial Job.

For who could understand it, who'd not lived it? The Monarch doomed to a round of Rubber Chicken, and myself doomed to a life of rubber accessories.

I've had an odd life.

I have tried to understand it, as much the Royal Monarch, as a universal, and unavoidable adjunct of Human Culture. The Primitive People had Chiefs; the Chief, being Most Powerful, got the best grub, and the best mates for his kids, and, one generation after the next, a Hereditary Royalty emerged.

Alongside these folks, it seems to me, we see the inevitably linked but sometimes counter-balancing institution of Religion. "Not so fast," these Shamans might have said, "look here, <u>I</u> have a direct route to the Rain God," or whatever 'handyman' was needed at that point of time.

"Let's fertilize the Land," the Priests said, "Look here, I have a Temple Goddess (Ritual Prostitute) (Fertility Bureaucrat); worship, copulate with, pay <u>her</u> and, then we'll be All Square. Well, we have Kings and Queens the same as Ancient Portugal, and we have Fertility Goddesses, and we may call them different names and consider ourselves rational beings, but what difference does a woman's beauty make when you are copulating in the dark and p.s. you've got your eyes closed?

No, we're all nuts. And never more so than when we ridicule our essential animal (ape) nature. Trust me. The guys I've seen, dumping their loyal child-rearing wives of thirty years for a manicurist! It makes the Versailles Treaty and the Dred Scott Case seem reasonable. Back to my life.

We buy the car. One selling point is its "curb appeal," part of which is its paint job, well and good. But then what does the salesman say? "Look how it matches the interior!" This might seem a reasonable consideration, but, think about it, you're <u>sitting</u> on the interior. YOU'LL NEVER SEE IT, save for those three seconds you're getting into your car.

So my life might seem odd—as I'm sure you're would <u>too</u>, if it ever came out in the wash—to those considering it from The Outside; but, like the car's seat coverings, I never noticed it. Yes, I made my living in a specialized (and time-honored) profession. I worked hard at my job, and took it seriously, but it was, and is, just <u>part</u> of my life.

As, consider, do you know a dentist who, however dedicated, goes to his kid's friend's Bar Mitzvah, and insists on examining the celebrant's teeth?

No. He may see the outrageous overbite, or mis-occlusion, or whatever it is, and it would not <u>occur</u> to him to say a word. Is it "withholding information"? NO. He's just "put it on hold." As I do, when not engaged in my work.

Remember, (in the Old Days) someone would be introduced, at a party as a "psychiatrist," and the other person'd say "I hope you're not going to plumb into my secrets!" Wrong on so many counts. As the psychiatrists (awarding them the benefit of the doubt) are no more inclined to "pry into another's secrets," than any other professional group. They're there to get drunk, get laid, argue with their wife, and lay the burden of their day down for an hour-and-a-half.

I perform for a <u>living</u>, and, when I leave the set, or dress and quit the scene of a consultation, I'm just who I am, and free to pursue my other interests.

It is these interests, actually, which have prompted, in those who know me other than casually, the suggesting that I'd had an odd life. I'll note my interest in entomology.

I was, as I've said, out on the Provo River, with Prime Minister Peres. His guards were stationed at intervals, leaving us, essentially, alone with the cold of the stream, the brilliant sunshine of the day, the wind rippling the most beautiful stretch of water, and the rhythmic casting, reeling-in, casting, which spread that hypnotic effect so well-noted by the various Christian Chroniclers of this, essentially meditative, sport.

As noted before, he requested of me a service in aid of the Jewish State.

That service I, readily, agreed to do.

I do believe I can relate it now. Neither he, nor the Knesset requested of me a "Loyalty Oath," or "non-Disclosure" contract. (I must say I don't understand the mechanism, for I've observed, as have you, this or that person who, having signed such an agreement, and being paid as agreed, has blabbed the whole thing to the National Enquirer, or gone on Public Radio to stand up for the Rights of the Oppressed.)

Heck, if I'd signed such an agreement with someone and then he or she "yakked out of turn," I'd lawyer up and plead my case on the merits, expecting Justice from a Court which, presumably, had the ability to read.

The Knesset (convened as a Committee of the Whole) dispatched me on that mission which one might opine, was to insure, for those years, the Jewish State's security from Iran's Nuclear Threat.

I was glad to help.

And I am in possession of a certain Award from that body. It rests in a safe, in a certain room, in an office not far from the King David Hotel, and I am very proud of it, as, though not myself a Jew, my father once had an Army Buddy who later went into the dry cleaning business, and gave him a (greatly) reduced rate on not only the removal of very stubborn stains, but on Invisible Reweaving.

I found that the Provo River was chosen not only for its seclusion (and, in a fall-back consideration the improbability that any occasional fisherman would recognize my companion as the Prime Minister of Israel), but for its offer, to this man, of one of his prime enjoyments.

Where he had acquired not only this taste, but his expertise escapes me.

There is this of his life, and, to a greater extent, of mine. Travel offers one leisure. This leisure may be employed to entertainment and diversion, or to education. That's how I used mine.

Additionally, life on the set is spent, almost exclusively, away from the camera, in one's trailer. I used both travel and trailer time in pursuit of my various interests, and was rewarded with a full life.

I once knew a murderess (served 12 years of a 36-to-Life Sentence), who taught me the ancient jailhouse adage: "you can Serve Time, or you can have Time serve You." She spent her time in what was, at first an amateur, and, on her release, became a professional education and practice in Diseases of the Equine Retina.

Prime Minister Peres caught now this and now that trout. [The River was, then as now, "catch-and-release," the only persons allowed by law the "taking" of fish, those demonstrating a genetic link to the region's previous (I believe they were Goshute) proprietors.] So he would catch the fish, and ask me to hold it, having admonished me, first, to moisten my hands. I thought it was a religious practice, and asked him of its derivation. He laughed deeply, and informed me that the hands were moistened to protect the (slimy but by no means unpleasant) mucus layer on the fish's skin, which was (how about this!) its immune system.

My hands being moistened, I grasped the fish, a practice I recommend to any who might have the chance as entirely delightful. Such life and resolution, pulsing between the palms.

"Now then," he'd say, with that residual European Accent, "Let's just see what he's been eating." He took a small bulb-topped syringe out of his fishing jacket, and inserted it, carefully, through the trout's mouth, and into its stomach, Drawing the contents out he showed me the particular tiny grubs the trout had been ingesting, and explained "this is what the son of a gun likes today. Let's see if we can't match our fly to duplicate the delicacy." And he would take the precise fly from his tackle box, which would look to the trout like its preferred meal. And so on.

This was the beginning of my interest in Bug Study, an interest I pursued for several fascinating years. On planes, in hotel rooms, off the set, while lounging between takes, and so on. In fact, I believe, during those years, I was (I was going to write "never," but, in the interest of both truth and a fading memory, I'll just say "seldom") not reading a book about bugs.

This came in vastly handy when, in Cocoa Beach, Florida, and one week before a very significant Missile Launch, a friend, (a part of the Space Program) began to complain of aches and pains in his knee joint. He was honor bound to report to the Flight Surgeon, and they put him through Every Test known to Man. They could find nothing. But the leg, below the knee, began to swell, his temperature increased, and he was THIS CLOSE to being scrubbed from that flight which would inscribe him forever at the top of the aviation world.

We were relaxing, or I should say I was, when I spied a look of grief on his face. "What is it?" I said, and he, for the first time, told me of this phantom and undiagnoseable affliction.

"If it can't be cured, I can't go," he said.

"Well," I said, "Let me see it," and he rolled over and pointed to the swelling just below his knee. A close examination revealed to me a miniscule pinprick at the center of the now proud flesh.

I took his pulse, and monitored his blood pressure. (By a method I had learned, years ago, in Taiwan, from an Old Doctor, ejected, and flown with her life, from the Great

Cultural Revolution. She showed me—but I will not tax you with the method now, except to say it involves a round stone and a sliver of bamboo.)

I examined his tongue, gauged his temperature, and asked "have you been rolling around outside?" He said, "Don't you remember, just last week, we went out seashell hunting down below the gantry crane?" I did remember. And I recalled the terrain, which completed my diagnosis.

"You've been bitten by a Brown Recluse Spider," I said.

He took the knowledge to the Flight Surgeon, who, at wits end, and puzzled by the Astronaut's medical knowledge, asked, "How did you know?"

My friend, not wishing to embarrass the M.D. by reference to knowledge which the man must consider "anecdotal," said "it came to me in a dream."

In any case, after the application of the correct anti-venom, the symptoms disappeared, the man was cured, and rode the rocket into history.

Fish Decoys

My fishing trip to the, now world-renowned, "Third Stretch" of the Provo River had a, to me, interesting sequel. I returned to New York still in possession of the "tackle" I'd purchased from the (excellent) Sporting Goods Store. I tried to dispose of it while in Utah, seeking out an organization which might distribute it to needy children. I was told that a fly fishing habit was more expensive than an addiction to heroin, and that any Needy Children in the area could do better with canned goods and shoes than split-bamboo rods and leader boxes.

I felt ashamed. Here I had exploited their country. (Much as it is dedicated to tourism which was then, and may still be the #1 moneymaker for the State of Utah. Still, I felt that 1) no money could repay them for the glorious setting of that day upon the river, and 2) I was there as a spy.)

My mother always told me to beware a "false sense of guilt," and I believe I've tried, over the years, to learn from and abide by her admonition.

Lord knows I've done enough Bad Things in my life— things, that is, which were, to me shameful, as they hurt another human being—not to waste morality in the pleasure of whipping up my own good self opinion through remorse about, finally, "the way things are."

I include in this latter category, as you might have guessed, Sex. yes, yes, we all know that one: I don't feel ashamed of sex. But how many (you and I) have given ourselves a "hall pass" for what we called Guilt about Sex, but was actually shame about or treatment of (or attitude <u>toward</u>) the persons with whom we were having it off? (Paid or <u>not</u>.)

The Mind, as I learned in Ceylon (today, Sri Lanka) is a nest of worms, diseased and maddened, biting each other to death. I'll send that all day long.

And when I got over my "rancor," at what I then called "being shamed" (how, I learned, at great expenditure of time and energy, can one person "shame" another?) I realized had not been Shamed by the comment of the Woman at the "Mormons Care for Mormons" booth at the Salt Lake City Airport. I had been <u>affronted</u>. Was my anger rational? Yes. Was it useful? No.

So I paid excess baggage charges for my fly fishing gear, taking it back to new York with the aim of selling it and sending the <u>money</u> to the organization in Salt Lake. (For, the woman, finally, was correct: how could an outsider know what the needy children of that area required?)

Which brings me to another axiom I learned in Ceylon: If it hurts, it's probably the Truth.

The truth was (and I came to his after <u>much</u> soul-searching, and, upon my revelation, I <u>was</u> shamed indeed, not by one overweight woman in an out-of-date dress, but by that much more offensive denizen of this world of lies: my own Mind), I was trying to get someone else to pay for my errors in shopping. I was, in fact, devastated, by my new knowledge. I didn't want to save starving children. I just wanted to save the excess baggage charges. (Which proved, in the event, to have been waived, after all, by the Attendant at the Airline Ticket Counter. We still exchange Christmas cards.) (And I was visited, I was going to say "just last year, but, consulting my daybook, I find it was six years ago! By a beautiful young girl, just come to New York to attend Film School at Fordham University. She gave me a card from her father, that baggage handler of long ago. I opened the envelope and read: "She could have been ours...")

To regroup, I noticed that anxiety about Sex becomes, so easily, anxiety about <u>age</u>. And don't they both have to do with the knowledge of Death?

My teacher in Ceylon thought so. he would walk barefoot, through a pit full of cobras, and emerge unbitten. (it was said, unkindly, that he made awfully sure to "walk on the stones" (by those of his disciples who "took the walk" without sufficient spiritual purity). But this was just a really bad joke. As I don't know that anyone but he ever walked through the pit. And I don't know that even the most malicious of gossipy tongues could find an instance where a student of his died. (yes, yes, there was the one case of an Australian, in 1959 who, practicing the Holding of the Breath, exploded after seventeen or eighteen minutes. But this, most sources would agree, took place during the Guruship of his predecessor. (The record still stands.)

Yes, envy was as rife in Ceylon then as it is today. It knows no bounds. Who has not heard a woman sigh with regret or a man with shame, on seeing, on screen, the you-know-what of several of my male co-stars. What was the man feeling but envy? Of what?

What was on the screen? <u>Light</u>. Light and shadows. Which portrayed (for the mentality prepared to perceive it) human endeavor. But imagine a fish, for example. The fish wouldn't even be drawn to LOOK AT THE SCREEN, let alone make sense of it, let alone, use the god-given organ of sense The Mind, to corrupt the thought processes and call it reason.

* * *

I took the (unused and barely used) fishing gear back to the sporting shop. Might you, I asked, accept these back (minus, of course, a restocking charge), or, barring that, say where I might donate them to help needy children?

A deep male voice beside me said, "Let me see that." I turned, and had my first glance of that man, a world-renowned carver of fish decoys, and writer on travel, who would (briefly) be my second husband.

I recall his apartment, full of crates half-opened and spilling out excelsior, the crates labeled, Kootkootchna, Talkeetna, other points in Alaska or the Yukon, which escape me, and The Barren Lands. What's in all those, I asked, and he removed, now from one and now from another, various carved, wood, bone, and ivory, utensils and figurines, carved by the Inuit (we would say Eskimos)—articles of such obvious utility that their intrinsic beauty, one would think must have inspired Brancusi (a sculptor). But what would Brancusi have been doing ice fishing at the Arctic Circle?

Well, my friend said, it's possible he spied these artifacts or those quite like them, in an anthropological museum in Europe. That was, I said, much the more likely (if less romantic) case. On one shelf of the small but cozy loft apartment were arrayed carvings of fish in various stages of completion: block of wood, rough-shaped fish, application of fins, several progressive applications of sandpaper, carving of scales and mouth and eyes, and, finally, paint. That is a great deal of work, I said. He smiled, and, turning off the whistling teakettle, led me into the bedroom.

Free Trade vs. Protectionism

I am not unaware that many of you may have bought this book seeking revelations about my friendship with a certain Elected Official. I will not say, "it is none of your business," for, if that is the reason for your purchase, you have done business with me. It is not "none of your business," but it is none of mine.

Men are poor creatures. They are deluded by their sex drive, and, in turn, deluded by and about women.

Women, which we know and they do not, are just human beings. Being human does not exempt us from the same foibles and rages and stupidities which madden men, we merely experience ours differently, with differing intensities and at different periods. The eighty-year-old man, he who once worried that he couldn't get his dick to go down, now spends his time in fear of death—his seventy-year-old wife, her time in toting up the funds potentially remaining after his demise, and practicing planning her day without the comfort (or foil) of her husband.

Women, however, are, in the main, <u>much</u> more generous than men. I have never met an honest politician, but I have, many times, met the whore with the heart of gold.

Think about it, in this oldest and (to the West) most corrupt of professions, here and there, we find a woman who accepts (and perhaps pities, and perhaps, in this pity, even loves) the poor benighted fool who needs to spend his pay on that cooze a healthier society would allow him to seek more easily elsewhere, and devoid of shame. So, then, perhaps, the Tart with a Heart, is one who gives value for money: the value not being, in the main, the use of her body, (which is all the man paid for), but <u>additionally</u>, and, as an act of generosity, her understanding.

On which note, I will beg the <u>reader's</u> understanding, for my postponement of the revelation which, *disons le mot*, may very well be the reason that this book is in your hands.

* * *

The Elected Official.

Yes. The man was my friend.

Yes, it seems he was married at the time.

You may call this "coy," as, "the whole world knew" that he was married. But consider, one in my, various allied fields of endeavor. Should we, the practitioners, demand of our customers, clients, or audience their marital status!!! How would you act, if someone asked the question of you at a restaurant? It's not the waiter's business, and it was not mine.

Yes, again, you say, but "you had prior knowledge!" Well then, you judges, lawyers, defendants, jury members, and consumers of filmed legal dramas, how many times have you not heard "the jury will disregard everything except the evidence presented before you"?

Think about it. You (or I) could <u>know</u> that so-and-so killed his wife and stuffed her down the sewer. Further, we could know that there is NO WAY IN THE WORLD he <u>did</u> not kill her; that there was nobody there who <u>could</u> have stuffed her down the sewer, that he was discovered in a locked room with the bloody axe in his hands, and that he confessed at length and in irrefutable detail, to the police. But the defense has had the confession excluded, the police accused of collusion, and so on, and so on, and the murderer walks free. Because the judge said, base your decision solely upon the facts in evidence.

It's brutal, and it's absurd, but it is the way we do things here.

Well, <u>I</u> took this admonition to my heart. And it made no difference to me the Marital Status of those with whom I concluded business.

That I may have "known" of their state, that I might have seen the wedding ring slipped "surreptitiously" off the hand (an event as surreptitious as the fire bombing of Dresden); or have spied the un-tanned space on the third finger, that space which, until the walk up the stairs, held the wedding ring; what business was that of mine?

And you may talk all you want about Free Love. (True love is, of course free.) The phrase refers, we all know, to Sex; and the circumlocution must indicate, to the wise, a lie or confusion. Free Love equals Free Sex. A "nicety" where none is required indicates repression, and some Bearded Gent might, <u>might</u> have understood that the repression was caused not by the Sex Drive, no, but by the euphemistic circumlocution. But no, "lay on that couch and blather on about your mother's $%#$," the Freudians said.

Well, they are gone now. Sex maniacs, all of them. [Believe me. They made reprobate Priest Child Molesters seem celibate. <u>I</u> had to listen to those Doctors' fantasies, their repetition and lack of invention damn near as painful as the men's appearance in their (invariable pastel) garters and sundresses.]

Let me say this about The President: He was the only human being who could make clear to me the arguments (on both sides) of Free Trade vs. Protectionism.

A friend of mine, an economist at the University of Chicago, considered my understanding, which, though it made sense (and perhaps <u>as</u> it made sense), I considered "too simple." He said, to the contrary, it was so clear that, in the next election, he was going to change party affiliations and vote for the man who was my teacher.

You can't say fairer than that.

Organized Crime

Which, and while on the subject of Presidents—and, if I may, while in the mood for revelations, and unable to assuage your (reasonable) curiosity about my Most Famous "Collaboration"—note that the peccadilloes of famous others, if they came to light, might be even more titillating, if not dismissed outright as fantasy. But silence builds a fence for Wisdom. While, I say, on the subject of Presidents: a since-defunct Australian Publication some years back, published what purported to be a note from the friend I chose to call Delores.

This note, "They're on to you, Get Out of Dodge, signed D." is interpreted, by the magazine's correspondent, writing under the name of <u>Wolon</u>, was misinformed, and shoddy. I was taken, as, I'm sure, are many of you, by the writer's nom de plume. WOLON, in Wagiman (the Australian Aboriginal or First People's language) means "grass."

Yes, yes, you Amateur Philologists will say, "grass," we know, is Cockney (also called Australian) Rhyming Slang for Informer or, as you would say, "stool pigeon."

A delightful afternoon in the Bodleian Library revealed to me the derivation of grass, rhyming with "kiss-my-ass." And, though unrelated to this inquiry, but of interest, perhaps to aficionados of language, note Kissimmee, a town in Central Florida (pop 28,767, 2010), which, by the traditional process of the Rhyming Slang, should have been the Reduction of Kiss My Ass.

For in the rhyming slang, a two-part substitution is offered, but the second, (or rhyming) portion is discarded. E.G. Bottle and stopper (Copper) is pronounced, not Stopper, but Bottle. Storm and strife (wife) is pronounced Storm.

Thus Kiss-My-Ass (Informer) should have been pronounced Kiss or Kissimmee, rather than Grass, but there you have it.

And I've let my Hobby Horse gallop off with me, but before reining in her progress, let me add a happy memory of my youth.

My father, who was raised in a saloon, grew up singing the songs he heard while waiting for his father to drink himself into a stupor sufficient to allow two of his crony boilermakers, to lug him home without fear of injury.

Through my childhood, my dad would go around the house humming or singing the old Tin Pan Alley tunes which were the soundtrack of his otherwise (I suppose) miserable young existence. I say "I suppose," as he seldom spoke of his youth. Thinking it, it would seem, as do we all, simply the inescapable way of the world. Which for him, as for all the young, indeed it is.

One of his favorite songs, and one the singing of which always revealed to us his more approachable mood, was "I Wonder Who's Kissing Her Now." Not a bad song, and one of acceptably wistful sentiment and feeling. But, on conclusion of the first line (the title) he would add, in a stage-humorist, "Stooge" voice, which, most probably some drunk supplied when the song was sung in the bar, "What's her 'now?'"

How odd, you'd say, that Ms. Ranger retained this accretion of crud in her memory all of these years. And you are right. But we are not at liberty to pick and choose our memories. Freud said the only way to forget is to remember.

More importantly, I retained the verse because of its recrudescence in politics (the theme, you recall, of this section).

I ask you to go back to the career of Henry Kissinger. He retired (so to speak) from politics in 1977, when Gerald Ford (a President) assumed the office on the resignation of Richard Nixon.

Some wag opined, "I Wonder Who's Kissinger Now." Not a bad quip.

I met him, as I think I've said, at the Bohemian Grove, and was delighted when, as it came his turn to amuse the Campfire, he did birdcalls.

(I recall the quip of one of the other Celebrants—the independently wealthy Bursar of a Large University.) He said that, on an early morning walk, he had come across Kissinger who, thinking himself alone—here he paused for effect—was Practicing His Accent!

Well, we laughed at that.

Wolon published what purported to be a photo facsimile of a note written to me by Sister (Delores). "They're on to you, Get out of Dodge." Wolon theorized (and it was nothing more than a theory) that my warning referred to the presence in the Convent of a newly arrived Novice who had been the close friend or mistress of one Jack Bosford (John Michael), head enforcer of the (Chicago) crime family of Sam Giancana.

Bosford, I knew only by reputation, was a connoisseur of fine wines, and open-wheel racing cars. He was responsible for many ice pick murders in the period 1953 (his return from the Korean War), to 1980. And was even said to have had a hand in the dismemberment of Jimmy Hoffa, and the disposal of the pieces in several far-flung construction sites in the Midwest.

The young woman, who, as Delores said, actually had a Calling, was troubled during the—sufficiently difficult in themselves—first months of her novitiate.

Seeking solace from an Older Sister, she, at length, surpassed the self-camouflage of false attribution (I feel I am unworthy, I once &*$% boy's %#@$, etc), and confessed she was concerned that someone was going to come and kill her.

Why?

Because of what she'd learned while in the company of her former protector. The young girl told the story to Delores, who told it to me, asking my advice. I told her to run for it, and take the girl with her.

The "photocopy" of the note was a forgery, but the content was correct. This fellow (I assume it was a man, but perhaps it was not) must have heard of the "get out of Dodge" note, and fabricated a copy. But whom could he have heard it from?

Delores was bound by the Nunnish (I presume) Seal of the Confessional. (Yes, she told me, but I was her Best Friend.)

That left but one person who knew the contents of the note: the Young Novice Herself.

She fled the convent with Delores and they parted ways in the Newark, New Jersey air terminal. Delores's last words, "get lost and stay lost."

I suppose that this young girl made her way to or found herself in Australia (a good choice), but that, while there, she was hard-put to make a living.

What did she have to sell? Her only skills (for she had fallen in with the Giancana Mob in her early teens) were a willingness to "get along"—her fortune but her face and form. And one more thing: she possessed information.

It seems likely that she either shared this with some new companions, as a means (we've all done it) of buying entrance into a group. Or that she approached a Journalist, and offered to sell her story. You may suggest that perhaps this young person was WOLON; and who can say she was not?

For writing is a trade open to all.

Birding

Everyone lies about sex.

We lie because we are insecure, we lie because we are cheating. In my early years I'd lie to folks that I met on the airplane, "What do you do?" "I'm studying pharmacy." Believe me, there's no quicker way to end a conversation.

There is only one topic productive of as much prevarication as that of sex. Would you be surprised to know that it is bird watching? Everybody lies about bird watching. I know, as I was, for several years, the confidential companion of a fellow very high in the ranks of that avocation.

Bird watchers live, as you might imagine, to watch birds. And, more specifically, those birds which nobody has seen lately.

That's what it comes down to. They carry a notebook, and jot down their sightings. How happy they are when spotting 1) a bird they have not previously seen; or, 2) one which nobody's seen—some bird thought to be extinct. This, to them, is the equivalent, I would guess, of climbing Everest, or of potting a black panther. ("Oh oh," you say, "they are protected. That doesn't go on anymore." I reply: grow up.)

If you think about it, what does this pleasure come down to? The "birder" sees the bird. He writes it down. He's joyful. Here is where the Religious have it right: he has experienced Grace. The joy was an Inner Experience. It didn't happen in the Wild, but in his brain.

I'll prove it to you.

Say I commission a replica of an Ivory Billed Woodpecker. Now, say I stick it in a tree. I ask Bill to go birding with me. "Oh look," I say, "what is that?" He takes out his binoculars. He comes in his pants.

He stares and stares. The sun goes down.

He goes back to the birding club, and shows them the notation in his "life book." Ivory billed woodpecker, they say, "That's extinct!"

"Ha Ha," he says. "I saw it." And perhaps he even took a picture. Everybody is impressed. He gets his name in various bird watching journals.

Why? So those who didn't see it can "catch" a bit of the experience. God bless them.

Well, these people are, I must say, (pick one or both) either charmingly Human, or Nuts. They didn't see the woodpecker, so what are they happy about? Pee ess, he didn't see it either.

And if he had, "big deal."

You comment that this is a harmless occupation. I agree with you. Except for this: Lying scrambles the brain. One thing leads to another, and there, at the end of the road, you generally are.

For, I learned, there are those that flat out lie about the birds they've seen. Consider it. They would put down, in their books, a record of some top-shelf bird, and swear on a stack of bibles that they saw the thing.

Why? To gain status in the birding world, I guess. But one lie leads to the next. And see our Champion, dragged from one rubber chicken luncheon to the next, telling the story about "how I saw my auk."

Pretty soon, he tires of the hypocrisy, but remains enamored of the attention.

What does he do? He ceases to remember that he made it up. He's just created a psychosis in his mind. And found it useful. Well, as we know of sin, it's only the first one that's hard. The Nazis for example, started in with lies and slanders, came to believe their own propaganda (don't we all), and we know how that turned out.

People will lie about the birds they've seen? People will lie about anything!

I can tell you, from my days in the Forest Service, wild animals are really good at deploying their strategies for attack and defense. We know the mountain lion is really good at pouncing on his prey. Yes. What he's better at is lying all spread out along the branch all day, and waiting for this or that deer to walk underneath.

The two are one. He uses the techniques of Conservation of Energy, to employ, to advantage, his innate ability to attack. We humans, similarly, predators that we are, husband our energies and wait our time: to get ahead, to get out, to get even. Since we cannot disappear along a branch, we use a different verbal camouflage to lure our victims close. This is called "lying."

We know that golfers lie. If you, reading this, are a golfer, I challenge you to stand before God, your chance of eternal salvation in the balance, and tell Him that you never lied playing golf.

Fishermen lie. We've, most of us, heard, and anyone who's fished has said, "He was THIS BIG," of the one that got away.

Well, why not birders?

Yes, they lie, and, yes, they cheat. And I know one instance where it led to arson and murder.

It happened long ago, and I was involved, only peripherally. But I will vouch for its accuracy, and you may accept it to the degree that you can credit my love of truth.

I have endeavored to be accurate in these reminiscences. Many may be beyond the experience of my readers—you, like I, may enjoy this or that glimpse "backstage," and I hope these writings may transport you, for a while, into that fairyland or Dark Evil Wood which the lives of others, on full reflection, are most often proved to be found.

The cynic might say "what does she get out of it?," as if his or her enjoyment depended on my intention.

Here is what I get out of it: the joy of reminiscence, and the satisfaction, if I may, of a Job Well Done.

Both Buddha and Ralph Waldo Emerson advised to stop questioning the other fellow's motives, and squeeze whatever diversion you can out of this eccentric Ferris wheel of life. One Birder finds it good to get up in the middle of the night and sit in a swamp. Another to lay abed til afternoon, and write, at random, the names of rare birds in a book. The wonder, to me, is that anything at all resembling reason and cooperation is ever found on Earth.

To return, I wrote earlier that someone might fashion the effigy of some rare bird, and, perhaps for a jest, glue it to a tree.

This was no random suggestion.

For I'd come across, as I hinted before, a depraved bird watching situation which came close to a crime. And that crime was murder. The birder in question, a <u>very</u> wealthy man, longed for distinction in the Birding World. His wealth allowed him to travel to remote locales.

There he would sight, or proclaim to sight, not only species previously deemed extinct, but <u>previously unknown</u>.

These variants (a <u>Transversely</u> Mottled Albatross, E.G.) he would report, claiming, in each case, his camera had malfunctioned. Ah, well, the authorities would say, "whom does it harm?" They answer was that it harmed the prevaricator. For, while his false reports were accepted (as he knew they would be) out of the universal deference accorded to Wealth, he knew that they were disbelieved. He became rancorous, and, like many another with His Lie, resolved to force its acceptance upon the unbelievers.

How to do so? By the only means ever known to man: more lies. The adulterer, caught in the circumstantiality of his alibi, elaborates, the very elaboration necessitating not only further lies, but the fabrication of evidence. ("Bill, if Mavis calls, tell her that you and I were bowling.") How far could this go in the case of birding? To burglary and attempted murder.

For there was cased, in the St. Johnsbury (VT) Museum the last known example of the Johnston's Thrush.

What birder has not, at some time, made that pilgrimage? Our friend had. And he planned to inflate his reputation by finding, and photographing that bird last spotted in the wild in 1931.

But how to do so?

He could, of course, spend any amount of money on a reproduction, stick it in the tree, and snap away. But here his wealth operated against him. For might not the Authorities of the Birding World, being convinced by his capacity for fraud, impute to any evidence the possibility of alteration? For what might not unlimited wealth accomplish—both in the fabrication of a counterfeit, or of a subsequent photograph?

No, our friend knew he would have to do better.

And here is what he planned: he would employ a band of robbers and arsonists. They would steal the thrush from the Museum and then torch the joint.

Our friend would then be able to plant and photograph the thrush, and, more importantly, drop two of its tail feathers underneath the tree on which it supposedly sat. Proof positive: his opponents shamed and silent; mention in the birding journals.

Off he went.

The plan, curiously, worked to perfection. The museum was destroyed, our friend received the bird, and waited for the fire to fade from fresh memory before staging his hoax. While he waited, however, he received a note. It was a ransom note from one of the brigands. And it contained a tail feather from the Johnston's Thrush.

"Put five million dollars in a gunny sack," the note read, "and await further instructions. Should you decide to hesitate, a feather will be sent, every week, to the International Association of Ornithologists, describing your hoax."

As you can imagine, he was stumped. He could not go to the police; and, if he were both shamed and found complicit in arson, he would go to jail.

There was a third alternative, and it quickly presented itself to his mind. He would seek out the blackmailers and have them killed.

That was the plan he set in train.

The very attorneys who supplied him with the names of the handymen who torched the museum had, it will be imagined, an even wider acquaintance in the world of crime. And it was short work to find those craftsmen sufficiently skilled to both locate, and then to eliminate the blackmailers.

Our friend set up a meeting with them at a seldom-used Hunting Cabin in the (REDACTED) mountains.

He came to the site early to open the windows, air it out, and make it generally presentable. He found a car and a delivery truck parked before the cabin; and on entering, in the lodge's one bedroom, his wife in the arms of the U.P.S. man. So engaged were they that they did not hear him walk to the mantelpiece, and load his deer rifle.

He shot them both, and turned to see, in the doorway, the crew of assassins who had just arrived at the meeting. The leader (he testified) holding a box of a dozen doughnuts.

On taking in the scene, they fled.

Fearing that our friend and some smart lawyers would try to divert attention onto them, they called the State Police. The cops arrived and found our man, at the kitchen table upon which rested a box holding the eleven remaining doughnuts, and one stuffed thrush.

The Much Maligned Pirahana

It was at the Franconia Notch Quilting Bee, one of those Tuesdays, that I discovered THE MUCH MALIGNED PIRAHANA.

The "Bee" was held that night at the home of X, a long retired teacher of Physical Education. She'd returned to Franconia with several of her ex-students in tow, and opened an "alternative technologies" hobby shop.

Though a member of the Bee, and a contributor in both supplies and refreshments, she had, previously, never hosted us. Why? As she said, she was hypersensitive to light, the result of an incident on an insufficiently anchored vaulting horse, which led to her exclusion from the 1964 Olympics.

But it's an ill wind, as she used to say; for, had she gone on to (a universally foreseen) Olympic Medal, she most probably wouldn't have had her long career in Coaching, and, in her words, "all the delights that that entailed."

No, she often said, she'd been approached by one of the two most famous of Breakfast Cereal concerns. In full anticipation of the Olympic Gold, they'd engaged her as the Model and Spokesperson for their new, upcoming breakfast food. (The working title, she told us, was Munchy-Crunchies, but, in her words, it is most probable they "would have done better.")

On her return with the Gold, she was to embark on a cross-country tour of lectures, in the pay of her Cereal Concern. She had already posed for the photo which would grace the front of the box. And all was in readiness for the career she'd been assured would be long and mutually profitable.

It was contingent, of course, upon her winning a Medal at the Games. Well, there was no question she'd win some medal. And scouting reports (by the cereal concerns) had indicated that the main contenders for the Gold (Belgium, and, of course, the Soviets), were over-billed—the Belgian girl sub-par on the take off, and the Soviet, as the scout said, with the grace of a bread truck, and most probably a man.

No, the contingency was, all then agreed, pro-forma. She was packed, and prepared to head overseas, her portmanteau crammed with the candy bars and deodorant she hoped to trade to the Russian girl for the nesting dolls her family and friends requested. But it was not to be.

This was a hell of a gal. She accommodated, through the years, many an itinerant athlete—not just those from the (great) colleges of the Northeast, but any travelling the Old Boston Post Road which stretches from New York to Montreal, and passed not three hundred yards from her door. [It, since, of course, long been superseded by U.S. Interstate Highway 91, part of the Eisenhower Interstate System; named for him (a source who "ought to know") as a consolation for his (not only Governmental, but matrimonially-enforced) separation from Kay Somersby, his lithe and willowy Wartime Mistress.]

She was known in the town as "Buddy," and a much loved figure, not only at the bowling alley, but at the Coffee Corner, and the Cheap Eats Truckstop (open 25 hours) (their slogan). She loved the town and the town loved her. Was it not the site of her birth? And had she not returned, from her Career in the wider world?

She had. And contributed widely and without stint to local good works, and charities, not to mention her tenure of 14 years as Assistant Chief of the Franconia Volunteer Fire Department.

But her eyes were sensitive to light. And so, she participated, at the quilting bees, not through that work (of cutting, piecing, stitching, binding, and so on), but as a Helpful Presence, mixing the drinks, stoking the stoves, and, most importantly, telling stories.

Yes, she likened herself to Samuel Gompers, one of her heroes, who, a cigar-roller, had begun the American Labor Movement with this simple notion: let one of us read to the others while they work, and all will pool and share the wages out equally. This was and is a beautiful idea, its beauty marred (if it is marred) only by Gompers' (recently established) continual usurpation of the Reader's job. There you had forty men; rolling tobacco in a sweatshop, and Samuel Gompers, drawing a wage equal with them, drawling out <u>The Last of the Mohicans</u>.

Well, you don't want to look too closely into <u>anything</u>.

In any case, Buddy regaled us with not only her stories and tales, but with her near-encyclopedic knowledge of quilting. Why, she could tell a double-Wedding Ring of Pennsylvania, from one of Connecticut across a packed Convention floor. (Yes, there were quilting conventions in those far-off days.) She could date a quilt from one glance at the stitching, or from the age (judged by "yellowing") of the cotton seeds found in the bolls used in the padding.

Buddy had never explained, and one never asked, the reason for her reluctance to provide her home for the meetings. She just let it be understood it was her "eyes." Rural folks, I've noticed, are much more accepting than their City Cousins. Why, who ever <u>knew</u> what went on in the Next Farm Over?

But "Molly," the scheduled host for that night's get-together, had been taken down sick, and, one by one, the other women related their inability, that week, to play host. (Kid with the croup, bitch about to whelp puppies, and so on.) Speaking of which, those Country Folk, among whom I was privileged to live, possessed a local courtesy I've seldom found elsewhere. For example, one might say, "I can't come by this Sunday, as Jim threw out his knee again." Well, we knew, and she "knew-we-knew," that the real reason was very likely something else. (In one case that the woman found her husband—supposedly mending the cream separator—having it off with a cow. And shot him.) But what business was that of ours? None.

To return, stumped for a location, Buddy was approached and, finally, stepped up, offering her Best Parlor, and it was there we went.

We came on fire with curiosity, to see the abode of one who (then as now) was one of our Local Heroes, returned from the wider world. The lights were, of course, very dim, to accommodate her affliction. And several young female heads were peeking around the corners of the ground floor room, young women, (they were, generally in their teens), who were being mentored or fostered, or however you put it, by this big-hearted athlete.

We were put into the Best Parlor, as I have said, where we found, laid out on the quarter-sawn oak table, that year's "work," and baskets full of the piecings and trimmings which would, eventually, form the quilt. (That year, a "Log Cabin.")

The pocket doors were closed by Buddy, leaving the room, and we heard her say, "Alright, turn up the lights, I'll stay out here." She dragged a chair outside the door, and was to sit there, through the evening, lobbing her comments, gossip and chat, through the just-cracked-open doors.

When she called, "Alright, turn up the lights." I began to look around for the switch. I found it, and the lights came up.

The group began the evening's entertainment, and called me to my place.

But I lingered by the light switch. For there, in the bookshelf, among the various tomes on physical education, was a rough hand-bound folder marked "Cross-Country tour—my speeches." I opened it, and found, typed, on yellowing sheets, not notes, but fully worked-out addresses on the topics Buddy'd chosen for her Breakfast Cereal Tour.

I leave to one side the question of whether the Company would have allowed her to give the speeches of her choice and construction. I rather think they, having paid her, would have demanded she "perform" talks of what they no doubt would have considered more commercial worth. And they, of course, would have been within their rights, for, as we used to say in Adult Films, "who pays the piper, places the pipe," a bit of wisdom, I know, no wise limited to that industry.

But what a loss that would have been for the Cereal Company. For, in reading the "sketches," I encountered a breadth and depth of curiosity and wisdom which, to, finally, make an end, was the inspiration for my beginning a career as a writer. At the evening's close, I asked if I might borrow the book. She demurred. I suggested that the essays should be published, again she, with the simple politeness one often finds in athletes, related her regrets.

After her death—a result, and I will never think otherwise, of toxic smoke inhalation, during her firefighting duties when the Old Mill burned; after her death, I say, on my return from Indonesia, I set out to locate her effects. They had been disbursed in an Estate Sale the previous summer. The Auctioneer had dealt only in cash, and no record remained of what-had-gone-where, and much had been confiscated by the Sherriff and returned to those claiming to be its rightful owners. (The true reason of my friend's seclusion, and I won't find this in Havelock Ellis: she was sexually attracted to kleptomaniacs!)

All of it was gone. (The one exception was her oversized litho of "September Morn." This hung and may still hang in the ready room of the FVFD.) But I sought the book—that book of essays, that book the memory of which has led me (over a long and rocky road) to the transcription of <u>this</u>.

What a loss. I recall "Decorating With Lint," "The Loch Ness Monster," and "The Much Maligned Pirahana."

I encountered two of her Mentees some decades later, now the proprietors of a bake shop in Oakland, California. I asked them if they knew what had become of the Book. They knew of no such book, having fled, on hearing of Buddy's death, across the border into Canada—fearing their apprehension by the Juvenile Authorities, and their return (as underage) to their homes, and/or incarceration in conjunction with a spate of break-ins to the area's summer homes.

But this is the nature of time. It goes by.

Fruitwood

I was asked recently about my decision to stop lecturing. I presumed the question referred to my absence, these last two years, from my Visiting Lecturer position at the Naval War College; but, no, the question came from one who—somewhat behind the times—had noted that I no longer spoke at "Woman's Forums."

Well, I ceased that some time back, as, with increased age, and some increased wisdom, I came to feel there really isn't much to say. And I was, I'll admit it, hurt, at what proved to be my last lecture, when I closed with what had been my favorite anecdote on the topic, and, on rising for applause, was booed.

You've heard the anecdote in question, I think, for it had some currency when I first began my career as a writer. And it was used as an epigram in Dr. Milton Fowell's (Nobel Prize winning) multi-tome on GENDER, ECONOMICS, AND THE COMMAND ECONOMY.

To wit:

I was a young girl. I was on my first date with an Older Man. After a rather good dinner, he took me back to his apartment and began, as what seemed to me a "matter of course," to attempt to loosen my clothing. Well, I was attracted to him, I thought his requirements not unreasonable, and, on balance, I was inclined to assent.

Before the "final act" I said to him (not <u>totally</u> in jest), "Will you respect me in the morning?" He replied, "I don't respect you <u>now</u>." I was deeply hurt. I refastened my clothes and he made me a cup of cocoa and said, "Priscilla, I expressed my disrespect not for your acquiescence, than which nothing could be more pleasant nor flattering, but for you <u>comment</u>."

Well, one thing led to another, but that is neither here nor there. His reply, and his kindness in (attempting) to assuage my shame is and was Part of my Past (we all have one).

I found it, over the years, provocative. Not in that I accepted his thesis, but that the choice was mine, whether or not to accept his attempts at solace at face value, or to build upon them a Hatred of Men. And, on my closing, as per usual, my lecture with this, my chosen peroration, and finding myself booed, I thought, "well, that's enough of <u>that</u>." As, like it or not, and credit me with wisdom or denounce me as a fool, I was invited to speak, and I defy the most talented demographer to find anybody on earth with more experience of men.

So, I said, I had said what I had to say, and the interested could seek out a fuller expression of my thoughts in my various works, and accept or revile them at leisure, and so I no longer chose to speak at Colleges.

The case, however, of the Naval War College differs.

A Rear Admiral, a fan of my work, had seen, he said, (as a midshipman he watched it, with his shipmates, once a week) my WOODEN SHIPS AND IRON MEN. The Board of the College extended to me an invitation, to accept their Hyman Rickover Award for the greatest increase in Navel Understanding.

It was not lost on me that they spelled Naval with an "E," and I took it in good form.

But imagine their surprise, when, rising to accept the award, I presented the paper I'd been working on regarding wooden ship construction in the age of Sail.

I'd become interested in the subject, you might guess, during my (brief) marriage to the Decoy Carver.

On our trips in the wild he taught me the various trees, and their properties: hickory for strength, basswood for ease of carving, birch for trim, linden for ability to hold a curve, and so on. (Interestingly, our guide, a Nez Perce, explained to me, as we walked, the spiritual and medicinal properties of these same trees.)

Indeed, when faced with the bite of the Brown Recluse Spider, not only was I able to diagnose, but, given the correct tree, I could have cured the thing. (The inner bark of the young Red Oak, scraped, pounded, and made into a tea, is both an analgesic and an antiseptic.) So, anyway, we walked among the trees, my friend seeking specimens for carving, (and, additionally, sussing out the rarer woods—the rarer both in taxonomic identity, and in grain: spaltered or burled walnut being so highly prized among gunmakers that a "blank" sufficient for a shotgun can go, on the open market, for as much as fifty thousand dollars.) I was fascinated by his discourse on The Trees.

One day, in Boston, I wandered down the dock, and found myself facing "Old Iron Sides," the *U.S.S. Constitution*.

She is the oldest shop still in commission in the American navy. Commissioned in 1775, and to this day, "manned" by American seamen.

I started comparing my scant knowledge of shipbuilding, to the living-before-me museum of Old Iron Sides. As my curiosity grew, so did my thirst for accurate knowledge, leading me not only to the extensive libraries of Seaman's Logs and Reminiscences, but to those of the shipwrights.

My initial lecture at the War College was on Nelson's triumph at the Battle of Copenhagen, attributing it (a bold move, but arguable) to the prevalence, in Denmark, some ten years previously, of Dutch Elm Disease.

So began my career as a Visiting Lecturer for the Navy.

After several years, however, an event occurred which made it difficult for me to return.

At the conclusion of that year's speech (the noted "Insufficiency of Fruitwood for the Gun Carriage Reexamined"), a

Vice Admiral took the stage, and, clearing his throat, said it was now his proud duty to correct a miscarriage of Justice.

Heaven knows how, but he had come across my application to Annapolis, and discovered that it was based (as noted above) on an <u>error</u>. He apologized, on behalf of the United States Navy, and, unrolling a scroll, announced that this Official Document was an actual and bona-fide Letter of Acceptance to the United States Naval Academy, with "all the rights and privileges, obtaining thereto."

I thanked him, and took the scroll back to my room. And I was, at first, sad. Here I had been baulked of a Naval Career. Through sloth or inattention on the part of a docent.

But, but, I reasoned, as we live but once, had I not, to date, enjoyed a different career, one I found fulfilling—and had I not, enabled by that career, expanded my interests and investigations into fields which, had I become a Sea Captain, most likely never would have been mine?

Yes.

As I so-reasoned, my nostalgia was revealed to me for what it was. It was greed. And as I named the thing, it vanished, and, with it, my desire to occupy myself with Things Nautical. I was done with that portion of my life. And I was free to use what Newsweek had called "her brain's wanderlust," in other quarters. Which is when I took up curling.

The Krii

How odd, I used to think, that I, a "poor student," have, travelling the world, acquired this "motley, unformed, yet finally alluring" assortment of interests and abilities.

I quote the above from Countee Cullen. It is a scrap of poetry I discovered, glued, as backing, to an Art Photograph of a nude African American Woman tentatively identified as Dr. Roselle Parkman, Ph.D., the first woman (of any color whatsoever) to hold the chair of musicology at the Sheboygan Conservatory.

I was privileged to know Dr. Parkman, at the end of her life, while she was in retirement in her "Cottage" as she described it, at Manistee, Michigan.

For, though of rough exterior, it was no "cottage," but the most orderly research facility—hand built by Dr. Parkman and her longtime companion Micheline-Marie D'Ardoise.

The "cabin" had been, previously, the bunkhouse of a logging establishment (Travers City Combined Lumber

Operations, formerly Central Michigan Logging). The girls had caulked and painted, scrubbed the rough board floors down to an attractive evenness, and lined the long walls (20m in toto) with shelves.

The shelves held musical scores, books, popular sheet music, handwritten notes, signed photographs of famous composers, and, so interesting to me, arcane and primitive instruments.

I'd come, after a brief but friendly correspondence with the Doctor, at her invitation, to examine the Krii—once an essential percussive element of the Indonesian Gamelan, long since discarded. The Krii would have been forgotten save for the musico-archeological work of Dr. Parkman.

The academics of the musical world, as querulous and vicious as any group on earth, had long disputed Dr. Parkman's assertion of the re-emergence of the Krii.

I read, for example, a vile ad-hominem attack upon, not her scholarship, but her Person! (A—to my mind—unjustly renowned Ivy League Scholar asserted, "I don't think she's even Negro.") The verdict of the Academic World pivoted on a pin.

The Doctor had, I learned from Mademoiselle D'Ardoise ("Pinky"), taken to her bed, after a "delegation" had examined her Krii, pronounced it a fake, and, in the "combined" (cowardly) report of the Investigative Body, asserted that they "smelled Elmer's Glue on the Sounding Board."

No, the Received Opinion said, the Krii died out in the Age of Sail, surviving only in the notebooks and reminiscences of the sailors. "Informed Opinion" held that it had been superseded when and as soon as the Islanders had access to the soup cans, which, discarded by the sailors, washed up and were cherished by the members of the Gamelan (Indonesian orchestra) as (pounded flat) perfect sound-chambers for the "motok," that interval or obbligato in the performance, previously the sole province of the Krii.

The Doctor testified she's bought the object (obviously of some recent construction) from an itinerant tree surgeon.

(Her "cabin" was shaded by the most magnificent Live Oaks I have ever seen. After the Hurricane of '99 I enquired, but found that they, the "cabin," the Doctor, and Pinky, had all been swept into Lake Michigan.) (A duodecimo copy of her SONGS OF THE PANHANDLE did wash up on Mackinac Island. Waterlogged, and falling apart, the bookplate of the Good Doctor was still legible, and it bore her signature.)

Asked to identify the signature, I travelled to Mackinac gladly. Yes, that was The Doctor's writing. Yes, this would be All That Remains of two beautiful lives, a dedication to Music, and an irreplaceable trove of musicological history.

The Coroner made me a gift of one of the few remaining pages of PANHANDLE. I've had it professionally restored (by my friends at the Metropolitan Museum, but perhaps more of that later), and it is framed, in ultraviolet resistant glass, and sits, on its easel, out of the destroying light, atop my piano.

It is the last page of "Git up, you flop-eared Mule." I've been told that when concentrating, wrapped in my own thoughts, or puzzled, I tend to hum a "little ditty." Asked by my co-workers the name of the song, I was brought then (and now, when I find myself humming it) back to my afternoon at the cabin with The Girls, to their warmth and humor, their expertise "in bed," and the story of their sad, sad end.

The Krii, of course, was genuine...who, knowing the Doctor and her unquenchable passion for truth, could doubt it? What would be the point of ginning up a scholarly treatise about what is (finally, and to the Western Eye) a pie plate? But the Doctor felt, as of course she would, a responsibility, to "music," and, to the Indonesian Gamelan, but to the Tree Surgeon who not only gave her the instrument, but set her leg.

Here is how the Doctor and I met. I'd followed the rancorous academic discourse in my travels, through copies of the various scholarly rags forwarded to me, in my "mad romps" (attribution withheld) around the world. When, there, in Djakarta, one morning, in that just-post-dawn cool stillness, to the reality of which, the subsequent appearance of the full-blown sun tends to give the lie, there, in a tiny booth, in the already-filled marketplace, was a young fellow, seated, cross-legged, carving a flat piece of wood.

I used the little Arabic I retained, and asked if he were making a shallow dish or serving plate? He smiled at my naïveté, and replied it was, of course, a Krii.

Well. I felt as must the Eskimo, hunched over the seal's breathing hole, not daring to stir, lest the movement spook the prey. I, casually, said, "Is it not true that the Krii is no longer used in the Gamelan?"

His reply, rich in the humor of those islands, is untranslatable. Thank God I had my Brownie.

My return to The States was postponed by the offer, from New Zealand Erotic, to film a series of short, instructional films. I had my shots of the Krii developed Down There, and shipped them off Express, with my covering letter, to Dr. Parkman. I received, as you may imagine, a (for the distance) swift reply.

I no sooner landed in San Francisco, than I again took plane for Detroit, renting a car. I drove to Manistee, and, opening the car door, was embraced by two middle-aged women, I supposed (correctly) to be the Doctor and her friend.

How to relate the welcome I received. The table was set with homemade bread (cooked in that Round Oak woodstove which now rests somewhere at the bottom of Lake Michigan.

The stove had been stoked with Apple and Cherry wood—I identified it (anyone can) immediately, from the smell, and commented upon it to the two girls. They nodded their pleasure at my appreciation of their rustic efforts.

They'd made gooseberry jam, they'd milked their one cow, and, from her milk, churned the butter. The fiddlehead ferns, sautéed in that butter, garlic and scallions picked from their own kitchen garden, were complimented by saddle of venison of which I'd never had the like.

The deer, I learned, was shot by Dr. Parkman off her front porch, just the day before.

"But," I said, "It can't be Hunting Season."

"Oh," she said, "you may be right, I must check my calendar." And she gave me a smile unmatched in its mischievousness.

We drank elderberry wine, made by the girls, from their own berries, <u>and</u> homebrew beer so strong "you could stand up a spoon in it." We smoked marijuana grown (in those Prohibition Days), below the corn which would, on ripening, also grace their table.

The talk, under the influence of good news (the Krii), good fellowship, good food and drink, the heat of the stove, and so on, grew happy and free. And, after a while, subsided—best of all—into that companionable silence so beloved by novelists.

The Doctor had a box of pre-Castro Montecristos, and we each smoked one (I swear to God the best cigar <u>I</u> ever had), and then stripped off our clothes, and crawled under an eider-down made from the very geese the ladies raised.

I awoke the next morning to the smell of the French Roast Coffee, and the sounds of the Krii, played by an expert hand. I rose and bathed in the cold stream which ran just beyond the woodshed. Below me, blue as you would like, down below the bluff, was Lake Michigan.

I could see smoke from the Lake Steamers, being funneled, up and down, through the Straits of Mackinac (connecting Lake Michigan to the other Great Lakes). It was hard to remove myself from this, so pleasant, thoughtless meditation (this deep sense of peace) contemplating both Nature (in the existence of the Lake) and Civilization, in the uses to which it had been turned.

I heard a wooden spoon rattling against a pan, and the voice of Bob (Dr. Parkman) calling "come and get it, you sons of bitches, or I'm going to throw it out." Smiling, I dressed, and returned to the bare-plank table, on which lay mustard-wear bowls and plates of the Civil War Era, vases full of fresh-cut flowers, napkins hand-woven by the girls on their own loom, and a plateful of coddled eggs, still steaming.

I looked the table over. "What's wrong?" Pinky said. I shook my head. "It's nothing," I said. "Excuse me."

Imagine my glee, as I left the two in (a very brief) period of consternation. I returned with an object wrapped in brown paper and tied with a string of jute.

I said, "It lacks only this to make the thing complete," and watched as Bob untied the knot, pulled the wrapping back, revealing the Krii I had brought them from Indonesia.

* * *

I wrote the first draft of the above while snowed in with a party of five polar explorers, twenty-four miles shy of our camp at McMurdo Sound (Antarctica).

The South Pole

You never know, and this is what I used to tell my students and those I had mentored.

I refer not only to those forays of mine into Academia, but to "master classes" undertaken—as did the Geishas of Old—not to impart the "most secret" of that art (most girls will figure that out on their own), but to instruct in the allied endeavors; those, in the West grouped under the (insufficient) names of Pole Dancing and Strip Tease.

Who can say that the inversions and grips necessary to maneuver around a Dancing Pole, will not prove essential to the rescue of a spelunker, trapped in an otherwise inaccessible crevasse. Or, in the second case, to "getting Down the Spinnaker," in an unexpected Gale—a gale from a previously unforeseen quarter, and of an intensity none of the (very grateful) survivors had ever imagined.

No, one never knows.

I bring to mind the skill of Pitching Pennies.

This I learned while a model in New York's fur district. It was my job to wear the things, pace through the office as if I were naked underneath (a ruse made simpler by the fact I often was), chat up the buyers, and, at the Bosses' nod, agree to go out with them for a "night on the town."

I saw a lot of theatre, and further developed that grip (mentioned above), useful both in "hauling on a line/belaying," and in the various manipulations of Brazilian Jiu Jitsu.

There's something about taking a girl out to The Theatre that drives men nuts. I made a (widely praised, but, to my mind, not completely successful) film upon this topic, BETSY LEARNS "THE METHOD."

There in the dark, but, faced away from each other, and toward the stage, the pursuer (the "man") finds a loosening of his restraints. He turns, in the near-dark, into a mere "Subway Masher," and starts feeling one up.

How I have laughed, at the writing of some middle-aged Midwestern Buyer—trying to, as if nonchalantly, maneuver himself far enough down in his seat, to thrust his arm up the (always) tight sheath dresses I put on for these occasions.

I swear, it was just like the first time a boy takes you to the Movies, and spends the cartoons and the first feature working his arm around the back of your seat. Sitting through Shaw and Ibsen and Eugene O'Neill and Strindberg was, for me, if for me alone, a hoot.

The rest of the audience were trying to keep awake until the heroine shot herself, I was entranced as seated next to me a member of Kiwanis worked to assume a "natural' posture while essentially down on his knees, and trying to look innocent, while working his hand, as best he could, up toward my *mons veneris.* (How much better for him—both at the Theatre, and for the health of his joints and lymphatic system) if, rather than attempting to maul a defenseless Garment District Girl, he had studied the more stringent forms of yoga. (Supdabodhakavasyna, E.G. could have gotten him into a more strategic position. And it is specifically linked to the health of the parathyroid.)

Speaking of arcane knowledge—what other sort is interesting?

I will return, with thanks for your patience, and apologies for the diversion, to the connection between Fur Modeling and my near-death experience, in an igloo, in Antarctica, quite near McMurdo Sound.

I was invited on a (privately funded) Polar exploration—the guests of one of the world's greatest (though least-known) philanthropists. This surprisingly young man had made his near-incalculable fortune through creation of a formula (today we would, I think, call it an algorithm) allowing him to predict with extraordinary accuracy, the future price of any stock. (One of my girlfriends quipped: "Imagine the size of his portfolio.")

But, and here is a lesson for us all, his complete success in this endeavor robbed him of enjoyment in two of the three signal pursuits of his life: gambling, and mathematics, and marred his enjoyment in the third. The pursuit remaining "girls," that season fell to me. I was enlisted as "the quarry."

Too easy, you say? For a—rather quite attractive—fellow not forty, worth all the money in the world...?

He thought so, too. And, applying to his one remaining hobby the stringency he imposed upon himself in Mathematics, seeking the thrill of Completion, addicted, if I may, to Achievement, he set the task of my conquest on a plane none the less difficult for having been self-imposed. He vowed (and told me later) that he would allow himself to "have" me, only at the South Magnetic Pole.

I would have given it up gladly, in that first limo ride home from the Prado. But don't ask me how—I don't know, save to say "I felt his need"—I decided, in the aid of, call it Good fellowship, or, hell, call it Adventure, accompany him on the cross-polar journey.

Well, two weeks out we were snowed-in. The gale "brewed up," and there we were in an igloo.

We had sufficient food; dried seal pemmican for him, dark chocolate for me. You may laugh, but I'd discovered, through my love for the Aztec and Inca "lost" civilizations of the South, that Pure Chocolate—any in excess of 89% Pure Cocoa, is capable of sustaining life (in the absence of other food) NEARLY INDEFINITELY.

As I had discovered that (reading Quipu), I wondered how those civilizations could be "lost." Quipu, you will probably recognize, as that name which indicates the Aztec-Toltec method of notation-by-tying-knots-in-string. The world's greatest philologists have all confessed themselves stumped. But I had something which they lacked, and that was a childhood at my Grandma's knee, creating the most intricate and elaborate variations of "Cat's Cradle." Could I decipher the totality of their knotted records? That was far beyond me. But I learned a thing or two.

The wind howled and howled. There was nothing to do, as the books had been eaten, several days back, by our pack of huskies, and he was not going to Break His Vow by fooling around short of the Pole. Rummaging in his pack he found a deck of cards. "Okay by <u>me</u>," I said. But, when it came my time to deal, I noticed that the deck felt light. I counted it, and, sure enough, four cards short.

"What about 'cards-in-the-hat?'" He said.

I was surprised that he knew this game. I thought it had gone out with the decline in the Camaraderie of the Old Time Rag Biz. In those days the manufacturers, buyers, cutters, salesmen and whoever was there, would sit around, <u>hours</u>, tossing cards into a hat.

That may seem puerile to you, but note that incredible sums changed hands. businesses changed hands. Lives were changed. All on the ability, or lack thereof, to throw a playing card into an upended hat, on the floor five feet away. I'm still surprised that any clothes at all came out of Seventh Avenue.

The Girls did not play. We, models, bookkeepers, secretaries, receptionists, looked on, when allowed, and shook our heads over the (to me magnificent) intensity of the display. The men would have bet their kids to turn their luck around. And more than once we saw a buyer, "going home clean," and (one or another of us) decided, mutely, to accompany him back to his hotel—to get him sufficiently tucked in and drunk to keep from killing himself.

A lost part of the American Experience.

I commented on this one night to a magician friend of mine. (Al Frosso, The Little Man in the Big Hat.) Al had been a state-of-the-art "Boat-man," in the golden age of liners. He, that is, plied the game rooms of these luxury ships, posing as a new minted Oil Baron, pleased to be invited into the poker games at "the Big Table."

Well, he took those rubes for many <u>and</u> many a score. Until the Pinkertons (the enforcement arm, in America, of Cunard-White Star Lines) visited him, in his lair at the Hotel Edison, and broke his arms. The arms healed as imperfectly as the Pinkertons hoped that they would, and Al lost that quarter-second off his chops sufficient to relegate him one and more than one rung down the ladder. He played the long- and short-con in and around the Garment District, and, as he became too well known, opened Al Frosso's Magic Shop on 33rd and Seventh.

The shop was a haven for the card-sharpers, pickpockets, magicians, con-artists, jack-rollers, counterfeiters, and so on, of Middle Manhattan. Al sold doctored decks, dice, crap and Faro layouts, rigged roulette wheels, and, more importantly, advice.

A friend (not I) came to me and I came to Al asking him how one might subvert a certain breed of wall safe. He got back to me the next day, and the information wended its way to one who could put it to use. (I was given an emerald necklace, but I gave it back.)

What a joy it was to inhabit his Back Room. And to be accepted as "one of the boys," was a delight indeed. For imagine the dreary life of a great opera singer, button-holed on every street corner, at every party, at a wake, a funeral, a wedding, and asked to "sing just one song." Is that Opera Singer to have no Peace in this world?

In my profession, similarly, I ask, could one not be valued (or accepted) independently of one's excellence in the Physical Act? And it occurs to me, that, like the opera singer, a refusal must always awake rancor in the refused. Who cannot but think, "Why not? It doesn't <u>cost</u> her anything."

There, in Frosso's Back Room, however, I was accepted, I say, in jest, as "one of the boys," but I amend that to a better and less skewed interpretation (as it, there. did not matter whether of not I was a boy). I was, there, one of the <u>Group</u>. What bliss.

Perhaps you, reader, have had such. As part of a group or endeavor <u>which one can not visit</u>. No, to be "in" the Military, the Cops, the Crooks, Politics, and so on, you've got to pay the price, renounce what—if you <u>really</u> yearn to be in—you must declare is the "lesser" world, and carry your share of the New Thing.

It's certainly like that in the Adult Film World.

And, no, the Life of the Set is <u>not</u> simply, "A coven of Bitchy Queens," (though every artist is touchy. You find me an exception and I'll eat my hat).

The group in Frosso's Back Room? We all let our hair down. If I could go back there now—the ancient plaint of Age. But, and this is the only, and a damn near sufficient, comfort: there was never a moment there we were not grateful. (I won't extend my rumination to a comparison of the Back Room and Modern Religious Worship. I will say that when the changed they Mass to English, my attendance was less regular.)

I loved these guys as the ultimate reduction of Show Business, reasoning thus: the Artist goes out on stage (or in front of the camera). She is betting her living on the ability to please an audience. In the last case, if she fails, she starves, or has to go straight. but the guys on the Street, they were betting their freedom and their lives.

There were two of the group who were (if dental records can be trusted) fished out of a landfill in Jersey. Why do I mention dental records? As most of the dentists I've met seemed to me bent. And if a guy is feeling up the patients under gas, or hitting himself with the opioids meant for the fellow in the chair, if he is tortured by a life spent looking into other people's mouths, this guy, it seems to me, would be a Good Candidate for corruption.

Consider this: "someone" is after you. What would make them stop looking? (the Mob and/or the Law.) Answer: if you were dead. How do you appear dead? Here's how: you get a bum into the dentist chair. You fill a tooth or two, and take an x-ray. Now you take the poor unfortunate out, shoot him, stuff his body into a landfill, and substitute his dental records for yours.

The bum is found, all his i.d. says he's you. The Widow needs to be sure. They go to the dentist. Voila.

But now I hesitate. For, though I've figured this out on my own, I know that nothing I could suss out has not been accomplished one or many times before. And I fear that my revelation of the strategy (as above) could possibly "blow the gaff," for someone engaged in a, perhaps, run of the mill insurance scam. [Note, for the squeamish: one could always take a pre-deceased bum (or homeless person), x-ray him and proceed as noted.] (In fact, I think this would be the far better move.)

They were playing Stuss in Al's back room, and, as usual, talking about Scores and Chumps. A lull come in the round of "can you believe this...," and I piped up with, the buyer from Afton, Wyoming who lost the farm, tossing cards into a hat. What kind of a guy, I said, would bet so much on a pure matter of luck?

The silence greeting me revealed my ignorance.

Well, they cleared the table, the boys put their chairs around the wall, and Al taught me the trick. (You can discover it, I'm sure, I was going to say "at the library," but today's world has more instant access to information.)

A bit of practice (rather hypnotic) gave me a yeoman's skill at the game. I tried to use my Power for Good (if you'll allow me). Thus: Back at the Fur Shop, I was cherished (by those whose prime vision of me was other than as a sexual plaything) as a sort of Mascot. My reading allowed me the position of Idiot Savant. And frequently, someone would say, "Look here, in the paper: where the hell is Burkina Faso?" And a supporter would turn to me and say, "Pris...?" And I'd respond, "Latitude 12° N, Longitude 1.5° W" and all would laugh. Fine by me.

And <u>once</u> in a while, someone who could <u>not</u> afford it, would be jammed up in the game, and down to the lease on his shop, and <u>I'd</u> say, "Gosh, what bad luck..." and someone would say, "Pris, change his luck, change his luck." I'd demure, and then be convinced into throwing the card for him, <u>always</u> though, proceeding my throw with the (naïvely spoken) admonition, "Only if you swear this is your Final Throw." And I would pout and bite my lip, and pretend to "gauge the wind," and throw his card into the hat.

So there we were at the South Pole. With a short deck of cards. And my friend suggested throwing cards into a hat. For Money. I demurred, as, I said, I had a talent for it, and I didn't want to Take his Money.

"I'm loaded," he said. "I'd rather not," I said.

"Oh for chrissake," he said. The only time I heard him swear.

(Note: when two-fifths of the dog team disappeared down a crevasse, he only shrugged, and cut the traces loose. <u>This</u> while they could still be heard, falling, and woofing, til they, eventually, struck the bottom at some incalculable depth.)

Well, he asked for it.

I told him the extent of my (yes, small, but certainly existent) fortune. And he said he'd cover me for any portion of that amount. We kept score on the back of a ptarmigan skin, using a bullet for a pencil (they're both only lead), and, as the cards fell into the overturned cap (seal trimmed with wolverine), my score mounted and mounted.

Caught up in the game, and forgetting his wealth knew no bounds, he became heated—always asking to increase the stakes. I was pleased that the play had distracted him from our (as it then seemed) hopeless stay in the igloo—a stay which could only, on exhaustion of our mutual stores—end in death. But I was sorry for his consternation, and began to "throw off," which is to say, to let him win a few.

With the change in his fortune his enthusiasm grew, and he removed the outer Igunkikuk, or sur-coat. throwing it to one side, we saw the four Lost Cards fall from his sleeve. "Let's change the game," I said, and we decided on Stud Poker.

Now his interest <u>and</u> mine were piqued. And I'd accrued a stake sufficient (through cards-in-the-hat) to make the poker game, it seemed, interesting to us both.

In any case, it was interesting to me.

We played for most of a week, at the conclusion of which I'd won a majority interest in Allied Chemical, staking it all, just as the storm broke, on my full house (sixes full of threes) against his (as it proved) four-of-a-kind, in which I <u>still</u> cannot believe.

Anti-Perspirant
and Roofing Tiles

Thomas Edison famously said that genius was 10% inspiration and 90% perspiration.

I was inspired by that quote to devise and attempt to market "Edison Brand Anti-perspirant." Undercapitalized, it, unfortunately, came to nothing. And I will tell you of another of my forays into merchandising.

Allow me a bit of history:

My allied professions required a high degree of physical fitness. You might suppose that I refer to the necessity for a correctly proportioned photogenic body, and such is, of course, required, and it was my study to retain God Given youthfulness and, if I may, beauty, as long as possible, husbanding this, <u>my</u> patrimony, as might a thoughtful trust-fund child (if such exist) her fiscal inheritance.

My concern with fitness brought me into contact with the world of the Gym, with weight-lifters, firemen and cops, and athletes of all stripes.

It was there that I met and formed a friendship with (REDACTED) (a lady golfer), which would last til her untimely death, some scant years after our first meeting.

Taken too soon, we say, or "the good die young." And perhaps this seems to be true, or, perhaps it is a "trick of the light," operating thus: the young, especially when we are young, appeal to us through their virtues. We find them purposeful, amusing, intuitive, energetic. We are drawn to another youth out of the mutually new-discovered happiness of a first adult friendship. Our young friends, of course, may have faults, and even vices, but the bulk of these remain undiscovered as neither they nor we have yet been tested by life.

When we are young our needs are few and easily met. The young persons of our acquaintance, dying untimely, are, indeed, more likely to be adjudged good, as they are as yet unsullied, and it is not that the Good Die Young, so much as that the Young are Good.

These were the thoughts shared with me by the Reverend (REDACTED), the spiritual advisor of my lady friend, and I have tried to hold them in my mind, cherishing, and, whenever possible, protecting the young, not from "life," but from one of life's aspects which hard won wisdom would identify as regrettable but not inevitable, I refer to bitterness.

I was inconsolable at my friend's death. (She, an avid snorkelist, was eaten by a sand shark.)

On recovery from my grief I was beset by a new bitterness: the project in which we were involved—hatched one pre-dawn morning on the veranda of the (REDACTED), a quite exclusive resort in Sumatra, evolved from my inability to play golf.

Steve was laughing, as she recalled this, to her, incomprehensible but charming foible. "Anyone can learn to play golf," she said, "you just put the little white ball into the little round hole." "All holes are round," I said. And this led to a bit of badinage, a discussion of geometry, a friendly tussle, and a dash into the surf.

But I was troubled by my inability to play.

For the game was her profession and her passion. She tried and tried to teach me the rudiments, but it was no use.

I realized that my inability was, of course, psychological: I was, I will use that word, "frightened" by the, to me, insurmountable similarity between the diameter of the ball and that of the hole.

How many, I reasoned, found themselves in just the same spot? This problem had been addressed, in the 1930's, by the advent of Miniature Golf, a national craze which made its inventors very rich indeed.

I realized that there was "more gold in them hills," and that I'd hit upon it.

There was an unexploited, <u>simple</u> adjustment which would bring untold new golfers to the pleasures of the sport, AND reap, for its inventors, a windfall which would make that of Mini Golf seem poor indeed.

I shared my apercu with my friend, and we made plans to patent and market the scheme under her name.

What "synergy!" She would bring, to our "alteration," as she called it, the passion which she brought to all-things-golf, her close acquaintance not only with the various manufacturers, but with the golfing Press, and her just downright flat-out charm.

I told her she could sell snow to the Eskimos, and she allowed that that was true. She, in fact, attributed her expertise not to her heaven-sent talent (though she credited that at every opportunity), but to her pre-nubile charm, which led the golfers of that club just down the road from the trailer in which she was raised, to take to mentoring her—supplying her not only with lessons, but with clubs, corrective dentistry, and trips to the great resorts of the world.

We were all set. She took the notion to her lawyers, and, through them to (REDACTED), the third largest name not only in golf products, but, under the name of (REDACTED), the design of golf courses.

The contract was drawn, and it was one which would make us very rich indeed.

We spent the time, in her home visits, between the dates on her tour, planning the bungalow we would build in coastal Oregon.

Imagine, if you will, the joy of "castles in Spain," when the money is to be real, and the nature of your digs limited only by your imagination if not by your taste).

At the conclusion of the Japanese Open she planned to fly home, having, in hand, one whole week before the next competition. But that was to be in Guam, and I suggested that she not expose herself to that brutal travel, but stay in the East.

Why not, I said, use the time to relax? Why not pop down to Borneo, for that snorkeling jaunt she had long been discussing? I would, I told her, use the time to meet with those Hopi Indians, in Arizona, who had agreed to create, by their ancient methods, those clay tiles we would use on what she referred to as our "hut." (Some hut, I'd say, 8,000 square feet of luxury.) A quip which always brought to her eye that twinkle which endeared her to the golfing public.

So it came to pass that we were parted. I went to a (as it proved) pointless discussion about natural pigments, and she was eaten by a shark.

After the first ravages of grief, I took stock.

I had my work, but did not feel like working. For how could I share either with my public, or with my individual clients, that which I did not have? And I had lost "a zest for life."

Well, I realized that there would be no better analgesic, than to continue with the grand project my friend and I had commenced. The money, at this point, was a small consideration, as it was to have been of use, only for our mutual abode.

But I thought the project itself was one my friend would have wanted completed. I could take the money, and donate it to the various causes she found dear (notably, Snorkeling for the Inner City), and the existence of our innovation, bringing golf to a much wider public, would be her memorial. The project would bear her name, and, quickly, in the mouths of all new golfers, become an oft-uttered if unconscious tribute to a benefactress.

I asked for an appointment with the Golfing Company, and received, through my attorney, a form letter, asking the intent of my request.

Shocked, my lawyer demanded an immediate meeting with their counsel. I attended.

There we found that, written into the contract was a time-limit. There had been one sticking point in the negotiation, and it concerned our demand for Free Golf Equipment for a number of disadvantaged youth. The Company at last agreed, but stipulated that the device was to be first put into operation within three months of the contract's execution, thus taking advantage of the publicity of the (REDACTED) Open.

My friend and I signed it happily, as our invention took no time at all to install. But, as often happens, that unthinkable possibility, that most remote and meaningless of stipulations, proved, in the event, very real and pertinent indeed.

The death, the funeral, and my grieving exhausted the time-period, and the Company, then, shrugged, and said we had no further business.

We were stymied, and we were defeated. I had lost all rights to our invention.

Time passed, the Open came and went, the device was not employed, and it became clear that the Company, now the owner of the thing, planned, not to release, but to suppress it.

Yes, and here is a bit of ancient mercantile wisdom: "the deal that lies, dies." I learned it in Marrakesh, and it has proved true since, and it is wisdom which aided me every time I remembered to avail myself of it.

Any two folks who want to do business should conclude business quickly, and, if not quickly, not at all.

For, when the broad parameters or mutual benefit have been agreed upon, why should any party tarry? "I exclude flirting and courtship, where the ritual is prolonged (though the end is clear) for enjoyment, and "the sport of the thing."

No, a change in the market, in management, who knows, a change in the weather, or the state-of-mind of one of the participants, a delay, and another, and then one or the other parties comes to consider the unconcluded deal an annoyance. Why? As they no longer remember the exuberance which masked the natural human aversion to take a chance.

Well, in any case, we learned the company meant to suppress the device they had purchased in perpetuity for (believe it or not) five dollars "earnest money."

Now, you might ask, Why? Why did they change their minds? I will tell you why.

The death of my friend removed from the deal the element of prestige. Given the pause, the company re-evaluated the notion and concluded this: that adoption of "the idea" would widen the appeal of golf, to the less-than-adept, but, in so doing, would lessen the (now elitist) previous rules of competition.

Golf-for-the-Masses, they reasoned, would debase the existing franchise.

Further, it seems, they re-examined the business model and were less than thrilled with the price-point of the new device. It was just too cheap to manufacture, too easy to improvise, and so, too liable to copyright infringement.

The Company decided to let my residuary ownership lapse, and, then, to play dog-in-the-manger, and count themselves luckily out of what they now considered an impulsive deal.

So the device was never made, and my friend's name was not uttered myriad times a day by duffers on their 9 or 18 holes. I did not build the "hut" on the Oregon Coast, I now had self-loathing at my inexpertise in business to add to my grief; and I was indebted to the Hopis for several tons of roofing tiles.

Well, life goes on. And, sometimes, it "goes on <u>and</u> on."

Time alters all things, and one of them is the non-discloser agreement I signed with the golf company. A sufficiency of years has passed, and I am now at liberty to describe the simple alteration which my friend and I contrived to democratize golf: enlarge the holes.

Trees

The War Poet, Joyce Kilmer (Yale, '16) wrote:

> "I think that I shall never see
> A poem as lovely as a Tree."

It was the memory of this, read, first, in a cold, rainy March afternoon in my schoolroom, huddled next to the clanking radiator—what a comforting sound—which inspired me to apply to the U.S. Forest Service.

I had been rejected by the Naval Academy. I was "at loose ends," and all my knowledge of winds and knots, of points-of-the-compass, and "heaving the lead," all this zeal and study, so it seemed to me, had been for nothing.

Later I found that, like Plains Indians and their "mobile commissary," the Buffalo, nothing goes to waste.

My time in the East taught me that one is all, all is one, and even the perfidities of abject fools and wankers can be employed as a Bad Example.

(I note the Inuit, who make the Arapahoe look like Wastrels from Yale, use actual dogshit. Dropped at those points where our friends would sink a tent peg, the excreta melts the ice, the Inuit then inserts the peg, pisses on the nearby ice, which melts and freezes in the hole, and there you have a solid belay.)

(Yes, the term is one from my early Naval infatuation. My fans have, most gratifyingly, commented on the connection between my nautical study and my "Mountaineering" film, A GOOD BELAY.)

And, yes, I employed the Naval term, meaning "to secure," as a double-entendre, and made use of my knowledge not only in the title, but in the actual filming on Mt. Shasta, during which a freak storm "bode fair" to blow all of our gear and supplies "down the mountain and out onto the Plain." That's where the 3-second bowline, and "immediate Clove Hitch," comes in handy, and you thank the Lord for what you, previously, might have mistakenly called "useless knowledge."

And so, there I was, wandering the waterfront in Annapolis, Maryland, shamed, and without direction.

I found myself in a (rather touristy), nautical-themed bar. The wind was whipping up outside, but I was not upon a training vessel—the Navy then employed old wind jammer as a training ship, and all the mids learned to "lay aloft," as it were, but I was not a mid, I was a reject, on the beach. I was not reeling from the motion of the sea.

No, I was crying into my beer, and cherishing my self-pity, when I heard two sounds which, in conjunction, interrupted my thought processes.

They were: 1) the rain battering in sheets against the window, and 2) the clanking of the radiator.

"My body's response preceded that of my mind" - this, I have, since, learned, the inevitable progression; and "thought," as my Buddhist Instructor taught, but an after-the-fact rationale on the order of all explanations of foreign policy.

I realized I had relaxed. I saw the bartender glance over at me. I saw him smile, and found I was smiling back. My "memory" had made me happy.

Well, we confess ourselves lost. We Ask for a Sign, but, more often than not, we're just not listening for the answer. Here is one case where I was. I recalled Joyce Kilmer's poem. I could think of nothing but Trees. And I went, at 8 a.m. the next morning, and enlisted in the U.S. Forest Service.

I loved the easy camaraderie of Forest Service School, and have retained, through the years, not only a happy correspondence with my classmates there, but the ceremonial bark spud awarded me by our Class Instructor, upon graduation— an award perhaps more precious to me than any of those given in regard to my later work. For they can be used only as a conversation piece or paperweight, but the spud can be (and has been) employed to strip the bark off of trees.

On graduation I was posted to North Wyoming, and the fire tower which was to be my home for the next fourteen months. I came with a crateload of books, the Savage, Model 99 30-30, purchased on graduation, and my longing for both solace and adventure.

How I loved my (forest green) uniform, topped by the traditional campaign (Smokey the Bear) hat.

Try fitting one on yourself, you will find that the top of your head is, in plan, an oval while the inside of the hat is round. I asked my Chief Instructor, upon its issuance, how I could fit the hat to my head. He replied, "You fit your head to the hat." If that's not as good as a Zen Koan, I will eat my hat.

Upon my fire tower I learned to keep things neat. I studied the texts and dictionaries I had brought, I learned to differentiate, at the last limit of my binoculars, a male from a female faun, a cold front from a warm, and to perceive the various qualities and virtues of the different times of day and seasons.

My frequent walks (up to twenty miles or seven hours, after which it was my duty to "report in") gave me an understanding of myself as part of nature. Learning to move in "the rhythm of the Woods," stood me in good stead, when, penniless in Benares, I set myself up as an instructor in Tantric Yoga.

And, I "learned to do with less."

I was originally concerned about my safety in the forest. Over time, I ceased carrying the Savage.

Locals had said that the bear, which possesses the acutest sense of smell, will "suss out" the odor of gun oil over three or four miles, and will stay away.

"Don't you want the bear to stay away?" I asked.

"If they stay away," I was told, "then you'll never see 'em. If you'd like to see 'em, don't carry the gun. When you see 'em, stay clear, don't get between a sow and her cubs, and they'll leave you alone."

I adopted the advice, and saw many (brown and black) bears, and did not regret the absence of my rifle (and its weight) until I was attacked by a wolverine.

The wound I sustained invalided me out of the Forest Service. (With, I may add, a lifelong pension. This I signed over to the Young Foresters Program, which was my first experience of the joy of structured philanthropy.)

The Service gave me the best possible care. The scar I retained was later addressed by the Reconstructive Team at Johns Hopkins, leaving only a slight but discernable, eight-inch-long mark on my leg—this eventually converted by Yakimo Kazua of Kyoto (may his shade rest in peace) into his signature "Esteemed Water Dragon" tattoo.

I killed that wolverine, reader, with the small Bowie knife I carried in my belt.

Congratulated upon it widely, I replied, in all truth, that I "just got lucky." To this day, I remember nothing between the snarl which preceded the attack, and my eventual airlift out (with thanks to the Border Patrol).

There is an homage, to them, well-known, in that most excellent service, which, from the filming of A SUITABLE

COMPANION FOR PAUL BUNYAN,[1] to this, has remained "our little secret."

Paul and his Marie, not yet revealed to be his sister, are lying in bed. She is concerned about her husband's drinking problem, and he attempts to cheer her by telling a joke. Here is the joke.

> A little kid is late for school.
>
> His teacher says, "You're late for Geography class. Why are you late?"
>
> He says, "I had to make my own breakfast."
>
> She says, "Sit down. Where is the Canadian Border?"
>
> He says, "In bed with my mom, that's why I had to make my own breakfast."

This is an ancient and timeworn joke. But, if you watch closely you will see that, after telling the joke, Marie (me) turns slightly to the camera, and gives a miniscule wink, which touching the bridge of her nose.

This was, in that day (it has since been superseded, which allows me to share it with you) a recognition symbol between members of the Border Patrol and Forest Service (who might, at any time, have been working "undercover.")

Thank you, my Comrades, for that helicopter ride.

---

1   As I write I am filled with nostalgia, remembering a gag from that film. Paul Bunyan is playing a scene with his Blue Ox, Babe. Paul says, "Babe, why are you so blue?" and Babe turns to the camera and says, "If he really loved me, he wouldn't have to ask." Babe was played by Richard Feuer and Rob Terqvist. How I miss them.

Chance, Fate, Karma, scoff if you will, but, finally, how otherwise to understand that (like it or not) furious, brief, mysterious set of interactions we refer to as Our Life?

Consider this. An eight-year-old child, separated from her parents, and lost in the woods, was able to build shelter, using only the knowledge she had gained in the Brownies, and a Bowie knife she found stuck in a wolverine.

And the most recent biography of Joyce Kilmer revealed <u>not</u> that he adored trees; he loathed them, comparing them favorably to the only thing he valued less: poetry.

Passing

It was through the auspices of the International Genome Project that I discovered my Maori Ancestry. And this was the impetus for my long love affair with New Zealand. I was in Holland shooting what many have acclaimed as the Magnum Opus of my Middle Period, WOODEN SHOE?

Production wrapped. At a celebratory dinner at a locally renowned Riistaffel-House, I espied that gleam in the eye of an admirer, that gleam well known to all celebrities. During the Floating Island he came to our table, a middle-aged, and, I thought (prophetically), professorial, nice looking man.

"...aren't you...?" He said, and I acknowledged, yes, I was. He joined our group and regaled us with tales of his adventures, as a young child, in the Dutch Resistance.

After our small cigars [the habit a relic, I learned, of their historic colonization of Sumatra (they kept off the bugs)], he asked if he could walk me home.

Well, I <u>was</u> home, staying at the hotel, "Dar Koenigsliche Gaasthuis," (now the Days Inn Suites, Amsterdam), which housed the restaurant.

I said I'd walk <u>him</u> home. And walk we did. Doing "the canals," the exterior of the Anne Frank House (then under—extensive—renovation), various squares and statues whose names I have shamefully forgotten. And so on, until the dawn "spread her rosy glow" over that so-interesting, ancient city.

My mother taught me, early on, "never ask a person what they 'did'—as that was but a shortcut to pigeonholing them according to financial or professional status. And I never asked the man what he did. He knew what <u>I</u> did, of course, but he did not, for which I was grateful, quiz me about the Profession of my Art. (One must be an Artist, and a Well-Known Artist to appreciate my gratitude.)

We talked of sundry things, and I-don't-know-what. Until dawn, as above. When, outside his door, I had the opportunity of expressing my gratitude. I have him a "peck on the cheek." Then, shaking hands, I noticed on his cheek a smudge of my lipstick.

My maternal instinct came to the fore. I moistened my handkerchief and used it to remove the lipstick smudge. He then asked if he could ask a favor. I said yes, and he requested the handkerchief, as a memento of our evening. I was happy that such a small gift could lead to <u>his</u> happiness, and left him with the gift.

We parted company, and I returned to Connecticut. Several months later I received a letter from the International Genome Project, headquartered, then, in Basel, Switzerland. It was from my friend, who, it turned out, was their chief geneticist, and the holder of multiple patents which, had he lived, would have made him rich indeed.

[I was about to commit to paper my knowledge of the actual facts surrounding his death, but "silence builds a fence for wisdom," and I, on examination of my conscience, found that my mumbled "yeah, sure," in response to a request (from the Amsterdam police) for non-disclosure, was as binding a vow (of course it was) as any quit claim deed, marriage contract, or lease. More binding, in effect, for it rested not upon the threat of recourse to Law, but solely upon my valuation of my own word. In any case, if I told the tale, no one would believe me.]

In his letter, the Professor thanked me for my generosity, for my companionship, for my insights and good humor, which, he wrote, he could only begin to repay (his attempt "laughingly insufficient") by passing on to me the fruits of the new science of which he—it seems—was the inventor. He had taken the lipstick and saliva stained handkerchief—the possession of which, he hastened to tell me, he cherished— his examination in no wise diminishing its integrity—and analyzed my D.N.A. (a term the meaning of which was then, to me, clothed in fog), to determine my Genetic Makeup.

His (handwritten) letter was accompanied by a printout of my genes. I found that, by percentage, I was two-thirds Afrikaans, the other third being a mixture of English, and German Stock. The smallest percentage, at the bottom of the page, showed .037% Maori.

Two-thirds Dutch, one-third German-English, and point o-three-seven Maori. That must have been one hell of a party!

On a more serious note, My Golly! I wondered under what circumstances that remote people met and mixed with my other ancestors. Historical, and genealogical research offered no answers, save the mention of a Coasting Trip by my Sea Captain Great-Great- (great?) Grandfather, from JoBerg, to Eastern Australia, Tasmania, and New Zealand. But how could he have gotten pregnant; and if he did not, how would the fruits of any union perpetuate itself among my ancestors?

Might he, I wondered, have taken a wife (wife or daughter) on the same coasting trip; and might she, there, have "gotten involved" with some fellow there, hiding her pregnancy throughout the return trip, her swollen belly attributed to "too much pemmican," or so on?

Aha, I fantasized, perhaps the child there born was of sufficient "Caucasoid" features to've been adopted into the family—passed off as the survivor of a shipwreck, for example.

Well, that was as far as my fantasy went. But it was not the limit of my interest.

As I was (according to the then-in-force racial strictures of both South Africa, and of New Zealand), thus categorized as "colored," I owed it, I felt, both to myself and to my People, to Stand Up and Champion the thing; which is, I here reveal for the first time, and will leave it to the reader to conjecture the shame I felt in having clothed, however inadvertently, my racial Identity, as, in the then-Legal Phrase, "Colored."

Well, Apartheid is long-gone, the Aboriginal peoples of the Pacific have been accorded full rights, and some (however insufficient) recognition of their suffering; and I have a whole "den" full of spears and boomerangs.

And my Foundation started a Hospital.

I received praise for it, but the praise was misplaced. Mine was an act, not of generosity, but of contrition, humility, and admiration. For until you've tried you can have no idea how difficult it is to throw a boomerang.

Little Sue

Who can say what is or may not be a failure—in what ways we may have touched another's life?

One of my favorite of all my films is MCWHORTER BROTHERS RESTAURANT SUPPLY (released in the U.S. as BIG-TITTED BIMBOS OF F_CK BEACH). Fans may recall that Little Sue McWhorter (I) was discovered in the back room cataloguing what appears to be a list of deep-fryers shipped during the last eighteen months.

At the end of the film, after the Sheriff has left; Sue, now in her dressing gown, regains her seat at the old roll-top desk. She brushes aside the various papers dislodged during the afternoon's romp, and, once again, takes up the Deep Fryer's list.

We now see, just before the credits roll, that the list conceals a Scholarly Journal. Which was, in fact, the object of Little Sue's attention, prior to the arrival of the Taco Queen and her Court. Now revealed, however, within the lists is, I say, a scholarly journal (a prop), named JOURNAL OF MUSI-COLOGY AND DISCIPLINE: THE DOMINANT CORD.

It flashes on the screen for eight frames, which is one-third of a second, prior to the dissolve, and the movie's end. The film "did not recoup."

After an embarrassing release in an Art House in Saskatchewan, it languished, eventually bought by an American distributor, and retitled for the American audience. But, again, it did not find its audience. (Though original 16mm copies today, I am told, fetch large sums as curios, or, if I may, Leafiana.") (And yes, that category exists.)

I am grateful to my Fans. I count myself among the most fortunate of Artists. Like any human being I have had reversals, and, like any public figure, detractors and enemies. Their scorn hurts, though I have through the years, acquired a certain stoicism.

I attribute the strength required for the philosophy, in part, to the joy vouchsafed me by actual, devoted admirers and fans.

And what is more delightful than to come across endorsement not only in an unlikely corner, but in regard to work one had previously dismissed (accepting the critics' verdict) as lacking.

I received a postcard on my XXth birthday. It was a menu a fan in Germany had spied, from a Wursthaus called MCWHORTER BROTHERS. You might say "it is coincidence," and perhaps it is. The fan, however, get this, was the publisher of a monthly newsletter called THE DOMINANT CORD, THE JOURNAL OF MUSICOLOGY AND DISCIPLINE. I did not then know that <u>many</u> musicians, historically, were into B and D. I know it now.

And I know because of the eight frames in an (I thought) forgotten, and, I still think, flawed work which died in Saskatchewan, and played only one weekend in Detroit.

Could we go back in time, I would go back to that oh-so-cold "soundstage," a garage, really, in Manitoba, and reshoot the ending of McWhorter Brothers.

Consider: I could afford to self-finance. I could hire actors and actresses to, as it were, "portray" those time has clutched to her chest; I would be free to do so, due to the loosening of those constraints under which we toiled in those far-away days.

I wound not have to pay off, nor to (REDACTED) the police. But would it be the same film? Of course not. Would it be <u>connected</u> to the same film? Only by my wish—pathetic were it not the essence of Humanity—to "try it again."

No, it is like the age-old problem of Philosophy 101: You have an old hammer, you replace the handle; later the head cracks and you replace the head. Is it the Same Hammer? I think what where' looking at is Darwinism in Reverse. The finished thing (the film) is reduced to memory, the memory to wistful longing, the longing to nothing.

The actors, then their fans, and then the readers of this very page, will pass into eternity. On some, planet, perhaps, light-years away, the photons which were the light which exposed the film of Little Sue and Her Afternoon, perhaps, expose it still. But to whom?

Bosco the Puffin

I began writing children's literature during my time in the Ashram. I'd gone to India (on the advice of a friend in Commodities Trading) to "calm my mind." And, indeed, it became calm.

The regime of rising before dawn, cleaning my cell with a split-bamboo broom, and my face using only the dew; the rough but satisfying food, and the absence of all external stimulation save the majestic spectacle of the Himalayas—these calmed the heck out of me.

I slept like a baby, and woke to each new day ready for whatever impressions that day would provide (knowing that they would be a) transitory, and b) essentially illusions.

This last did not hold true of the appearance of the (REDACTED) rebels. Or, better, their rapine and pillage may have been an illusion, but it sure as hell felt real to me.

I don't know how it was that I was elected to negotiate with them, but elected I was.

(I've often notices this pre-verbal, communal deci-
sion-making in ad-hoc groups. See the poor passengers,
moored at the Baggage Carousel, hour after hour, awaiting
their bags. Should an Airline Representative appear, inevitably one of the passengers will, after some initial exchange,
become the spokesperson for all.)

It may be, case-by-case, the tallest, most outspoken,
angriest, and so on, but in every case, the "herd" will have
been found to have made a choice. In the case of the Brigands,
that choice fell upon me.

The negotiations (who would die as a religious sacrifice,
who would die "just for the hell of it;" and who would be
likely as a candidate for ransom, who would be debauched,
et cetera), proceeded through the twilight hours, and into
the night.

Talks were conducted in a mixture of English, pidgin-
German (closely allied to Afrikaans, and a survival, in those
mountains, of the German Military Expeditions of the Second
World War), and sign language. The final sticking point
occurred when the Chief Brigand, informed that he'd just
smoked the last of the American cigarettes, became enraged,
struck off the head of a pig with his *Yatagan*, and screamed
immediate vengeance upon the entire group.

"I see much merit in your position," I communicated to
him, "and you'd be totally within your rights to, as you said,
'disembowel us and throw us down the gorge,' but, if I might,
remember our talks about possible ransom, not to mention

the International Good Will you'd gain from engaging in a reasonable, Capitalist exchange."

His eyes gleamed. I did not like his smile. He rubbed his hands, and I was to discover the man's profoundest vice: he was addicted, not primarily to violence, but to <u>gambling</u>.

His "invasion," in fact, preceded from a taunt by his brother-in-law, in effect: "betcha you can't destroy that Monastery and be back by Breakfast." (I do not know the stakes involved.)

In any case, the Chief Brigand rubbed his hands and proposed, to me, a wager. He would, as he said, "take my weak-Western suggestion, and add some interest to it."

"I'm listening," I said.

He then proposed to wager the lives and the persons, and the residual physical integrity of the monastery, on a game of chance.

Heads or tails, he said; heads you go home, tails we send you to hell. I'll take that wager, I said, but will call your attention to the ancient (and near-universal) Code Duello, by which I mean, as you have proposed the challenge, it is to <u>me</u> to choose the means.

He took some counsel with his supporters, then returned to me, and agreed. "What is it you propose?" he said.

I told him we would play "Rock, Paper, Scissors." (A game at which I do not believe I had ever been beaten.)

I was anxious, only that the game be known to him, and indeed it was (as, I have found, it is, in every locale and civilization in which I remember to ask the question. (The Brigands knew it as "a goat, my cousin, and the sheep.)

The yogis, and the brigands formed a circle. The Robber Chief uttered some shrill incantations, which absorbed a full quarter-hour. Then he turned to me.

The priest struck the ancient brass gong, once, twice, thrice, and, on the third strike, the vandal and I threw out our hands.

I had my eyes locked on his, and did not receive (the anticipated) knowledge of my victory, first, from his <u>eyes</u> (the usual messenger) but from the sharp intake of the gathered brigands' breath. Their chief looked down to see that my Rock (the Cousin) had defeated his Scissors (the Goat), as it does, all over the world.

He then (and it is here that I lost my respect for him) uttered that well-known and pathetic suggestion of the welsher: "Two out of three..." My look of disappointment and scorn was enough to cause him to lower his eyes. He and his Band melted away.

But the usual unaligned, unattached, and meditative routine of the Monastery had been ruptured.

The Yogis, the Monks, the Visitors, devolved from a silent group of Seekers After Truth, into a chattering bunch of gossips. And it sounded like a Tupperware party.

Well, I was not to be retrieved (by donkey) for three days; it was obvious that the monastery would take much longer than that to calm down, even given the (heroic) consumption both of ceremonial rice wine, and of Bhang.

But I—who could, and would, and of course did, party vehemently, had come for a different realm of experience—had no wish to see a bunch of monks playing what turned out to be a tantric form of Strip Poker. (My goodness, they looked like convention goers at the Palmer House.)

So I took to my room. I looked at the mountains, but my reverie was broken.

No, I commend myself on few things. (You may riposte, "No, Leafy, no," but be assured I know my fault better than you could. Thank God.)

Chief among my virtues is my Use of Time.

I would not call it a "work ethic," as I don't know that it's an ethic at all. But I hate being non-productive.

My stay at the Ashram was productive of peace. Now that was gone, and what was I to do?

I began to write. Why? I couldn't tell you. How did I choose my subject? I don't know. Why this rather than that? It's beyond me. But I began to write a book about a puffin.

On my return to the States I (never reluctant to ask someone for help, I'm glad to give it, and I feel entitled to ask for it) (and I'm prepared to "take no for an answer") had contacted Howard Leslie Broone, who agreed to read the book, and, reading it, contributed the illustrations (they came by return mail, with a note which modesty requires I treasure in privacy).

The royalties from my children's book have supported the reconstruction of the monastery, and the sentiments of young and old readers continues to cheer me, as a new generation has come to appreciate that rascal's antics.

The Greasy Pole

I am going through my notes. I suppose this presages a change of some sort, indeed, I'm sure it does. We all know the evenings spent, rummaging through the attic, basement or garage, which precede a change. Be it a move, a marriage, a divorce, we'll find ourselves, then, going through boxes.

Looking for what? I call it The Human Search for Meaning. That's right. And in that search, though we might call it by a different name, we do find meaning.

How do I know? I'll prove it to you: we conclude the search. That's what we do when we locate our lost car keys, or the pair to the elbow-length glove or gauntlet. We stop looking. And that's what we do in Our Search For Meaning. Stop, because we've found it.

Now, we might not be able to put it into words, but it's there nonetheless, calling itself resignation, perhaps, or perhaps peace, or (and I find this often) bemusement at The Human Condition. (Mine.)

I was about to set out on what I thought would be a several-month-long shoot in a country which I'll leave unnamed. It turned out this was the beginning of what more than one biographer has referred to as "Her Lost Year."

That is a story for another day.

But there I was, in the old cedar-lined attic of the Summer Cottage—my prized and beloved retreat and refuge—digging around in old files. They held the notes and journals upon which I have relied for whatever accuracy this book might contain. (The files now rest in my archive at the University of Oklahoma.)

The notes were, as the situation allowed, written on fine laid-vellum notebooks, from the finest shops on Bond Street; scribbled on matchbooks, transcribed, in dark purple ink, in the copperplate handwriting of "the old Indian Babu," of the British Empire. (I still correspond with his grandchildren! One is a gynecologist in Poona, and the twins play soccer for Manchester United.)

Several are written on birchbark, using, for ink, a mixture of crushed juniper berries and blood. One is scribbled on the back of the Program of the June 18th, 19xx Idaho State Fair. It is a reminder to send thanks to the head of a village in the Amazon.

I wrote that letter. It was a note of thanks, for he had given me the means to save a person's life.

I'd been invited to the Fair to judge The Greasy Pole. To this day, I do not know whether or not the judges intended this as a double-entendre. I am inclined to think that they did not. For they were as upright, as you'd wish farmers to be—as they must be, dealing, as they do, so directly with the Forces of Nature.

That was one heck of a fair. The date of The Competitions had been chosen as carefully as (of old) was the Wedding Day of the Young Virgin—the Wise Women calculating to insure that the nuptials did not coincide with The Time of the Month. Where are those days now? They are gone. I've been invited to so many destination weddings that I-don't-know-what.

Now, here I will insert that phrase which, if not the first signal of increase of knowledge, is, certainly, the far-off but discernible welcoming wave of Death: in the old days.

In the old days the wedding was celebrated as the Pagan Feast it was. The Girl's family rejoiced at getting her safely off their hands—they no longer had to either feed her or protect her honor with sharp instruments and bludgeons. The Boy celebrated the removal of her panties, and his family rejoiced that they weren't paying for the thing.

Everyone got to participate in celebrating the girl's upcoming defloration. Most, save the groom, of course, only through drunkenness, ribald jokes, and, on the part of the men, barely controllable fantasy—remove the element of sexual anticipation so pressing even its legitimacy could not lessen it—remove that, I say, and what have you got? Theme Weddings, Travel to the Mountains, The Shore, and Amusement Parks.

The dates of the State Fair competitions, as above, was chosen with care, and the pains in its choice justified by the high, clear, (low humidity), bright June day.

The lack of humidity, I was told, figured to no small extent, in the record—set that year—of the Greasy Pole Climb. Humidity, I learned affects the viscosity of hog lard. (How could it not?!)

My office as Judge of that competition was, largely ceremonial. The winner would be he (no girls participated in those days) who first contrived to climb the pole, and retrieve, from its top, the upturned lard bucket.

Well, you might wonder, wouldn't those picked to go first have an advantage? Yes and no. For, though they'd get First Chance, they were hindered by the fresh-greased condition of the pole.

Was not the pole re-greased after each attempt, you might ask. No, it was not. That each subsequent climb decreased (slightly) the grease on the pole, offset directly, the potential benefits of precedence.

I often wondered if this were a function of chance, of undigested experience, or of deep wisdom on the part of the competition's creators. I discussed this once with a (famed) mathematician from the Jet Propulsion Laboratories of Pasadena. In his reply, "That's a good one," I was pleased to discern the humor one employs only with a co-initiate.

(Not that I'm good at math. But that I tend to think about things.)

The Order of the Competitions put the Calf Judging first, the Greasy Pole last. In between came the House of Hay [awards for the Largest, Most Traditional, Most Inventive structures built of that commodity (no glue allowed)], the Hog-Weighing Contest, the Tug of War, Pie Judging, Pie Eating, Most Tasty Preserve, and the Greasy Pole.

So my day, as you can see, was, until near sundown, free of responsibility. Additionally, as a judge, I was accorded Front Row Seats for each of the events.

As a Judge, as a Visitor, and, yes, as an Attractive Woman, I had pressed on me, throughout the day, that Lemonade of which I have never found the equal.

I persisted, ladylike, in keeping my seat, through the Pie Judging contest. [Each woman had to enter two pies, one for the judging, and a second, to be used in the subsequent competition (the pie eating.)] Great was the anticipation, as each of the farm women, dressed in her Sunday Best, came forth, to stand before her offering.

I can see them now. They were all large women. Farm women, capable and strong able to deliver a calf at four a.m., or help in a neighbor's childbirth. They had sent their men and boys off to war, and carried on when they did not return. They'd weathered frost and snow, tornadoes and floods, and now were engaged in that pastime so dear to the country which they built: eating fruit pies.

How fine, I mused, that these, who'd looked on, stoical, and coolly, in any and each emergency, now trembled before the (finally subjective) verdict of the Judge of Pies.

I had to pee.

I'll tell you I was glad of the excuse, for though I had not tasted the pies, I had seen the women. And they all looked worthy. I was thankful that it was not I who had to make the choice. For I could award the Crown but to one, and would, thus, bestow upon the rest disappointment.

Returning from relief [I'll confess, while in That Place I'd smoked a cigarette. Yes, many women at the Fair were smoking, but I felt that my position entailed upon me a somewhat higher (or, if you will, more staid, or Old Fashioned) sort of conduct.], I encountered the scene described below.

I'd quitted the dais during the last pie, and so, figured to miss the beginning of the Pie Eating.

On walking back toward the reviewing stand I heard screams and the calls for a doctor. Regaining the stand I saw, below me, a very fat man, stretched out rigid on the ground.

Miniscule convulsions, I saw, wracked his frame, damped by the high starch in his overalls.

Several men were fidgeting around him, loosening clothes, chafing his wrists, and generally at a loss.

"What happened?" I asked.

"He was eating his third Huckleberry," I was told, "and he ingested a bee."

Well, the answer was clear. He was in anaphylactic shock. That was plain as day, and would be clear to any doctor coming on the scene.

Many in the crowd, and I on the stand, scanned the area, for the appearance of that doctor whose summons rang on every lip.

There was no doctor and the man was getting worse, as I shouldered aside the onlookers on the stair, and cried to the fattest man, "Give me your belt," and to the women, "Give me your hatpins!"

The tone of my command compelled immediate compliance, and I took my tools and bent over the unfortunate contestant. I applied that remedy so well known in that nesting-ground of the world's most poisonous insects. (How could they have survived otherwise?)

The man convulsed, I turned him on his side, he expelled the bee, and, believe it or not, after a brief interval, he was allowed to continue in the competition. (With the penalty of one extra half-a-pie, in reference to his time-elapsed away from the table.)

My note to the Amazon Chief was written that evening, at the Sing Along. For though the crowd concluded that Happy Day in Song, I was overcome with a sort of wistful wonder. Why, I mused, had fate put me, first, twelve hundred miles from that which we call Civilization, and taught me, in that "uncivilized" spot, a simple folk remedy known in those jungles for millennia, but of which Western Science was completely ignorant? And then (speaking of Fate) why had she placed me, in possession of that knowledge, in the only spot enabling me to save the farmer's life? (For, had I not been a Judge, I would not have had a place on the podium above the misfortune; and had I been merely a spectator returning from the loo, I'd have been at the back of the crowd and never would have observed, let alone diagnosed, the fellow's trouble.)

I wrote in my Pidgin-Portuguese (not that different from Spanish, really, when written—when they're, however, speaking, who the hell knows what they mean), to a "special friend of mine," a note was addressed to a Prelate in Sao Paulo, with my request that he forward it, "up the river," as we said, to its final recipient.

At my hotel, I transcribed the note, and, the next morning, took the transcription down to Western Union. It was sent to my friend by telegram, and, thence, by seaplane, riverboat, runner, and, eventually, canoe, to that most remote of locations.

Acknowledgment I received none, nor could I hope to have done so.

The true link with the Amazon came at the moment of my application of the Home Remedy—human knowledge setting at nothing the supposed vastnesses of space and time.

The Farmer sent me a very handsome appreciation, and a braided horsehair hatband which, from that day to this, has adorned my Stetson. (The particulars of my trip to the Amazon may be found at The University of Oklahoma.)

The Spanking Paddle
and The Song of the Whale

(Originally: Doors Science Was Not Meant to Open)

I've often been asked "what was your most unusual experience?" Well, my life has been a varied one, and what any or most listeners might have deemed "unusual" was, likely, for me, the normal course of events.

In the Sex Trade, as in any business, there are only "just so many ways it can be done;" additionally, though variations of deception or perfidy are limitless, their basic categories are few, and the capacity to be surprised by malefaction, over time, becomes as diminished as that of wonder at a body type's deformation or, indeed, perfection.

Well, the sad, and inevitable disillusion at the Evil Ways of the World is of course offset by wonder at unlooked-for revelations of virtue, and I am blessed to have encountered many.

But my fans, inquiring about my Most Unusual Experience, do not wish, I am sure, to be told of this or that unselfishness or act of courage. They are looking for the shocking and outré.

I will not disappoint them.

* * *

In 19xx I had formed an informal alliance with a (REDACTED) sub-group of the American Psychoanalytic Association. Our connection sprang from a chance encounter at one of the group's bi-annual conclaves in Boca Raton.

"What Freud had right," I said, "was that we suffer trauma. What he had wrong is that we can cure it through bitching." I knew a better cure, and shared it with them: Spanking.

"Yes," I told them, "Spanking. It has fallen out of favor as a means of correcting the young, but it's just as effective now as always in the cleansing of the mind.

"You don't have," I told them, "to dress up in corsets, or get some Professional to wear a leather mask, no."

And I removed from its case the therapeutic instrument several of the men had seen in quite another setting. It was a *chi-hwan* or "correction paddle" from the Ming Dynasty.

Fashioned in a dark, close-grained wood, its handle culminates in a trefoil, rather than the usual (and more utilitarian)) "rattail." This, I explained, identifies it as an instrument of what we, today, might call Bondage and Discipline (the other, simpler form, indicating an everyday torturer's tool.)

"Yes, spank them," I said, "and watch what happens."

In my experience what happens is this: the patient, rather than being encouraged in rage against people long dead or moved to Florida, is <u>physically</u> induced to change the object of dissatisfaction from his mother to himself.[2]

"Yes," I explained, "See here the blessed force of auto suggestion. Its province should not be that of the stage hypnotists in the lounges of Las Vegas, convincing some tire salesman from Toledo that he is a carp. No. It is a therapeutic tool."

"Get someone to request to be beaten, and, with the first blow, his <u>body</u> will convince him that 'he has been bad.'"

How would this alleviate suffering? I was asked. And I responded with that Georgian nautical catch-phrase so well-known to the foremast sailors of the British Navy in the fighting age of sail, "punishment cancels crime."

Now, I said, see how simple: A man is troubled (by guilt, by shame, or, equally, by sexual longing). He is incapable of bringing his conscious mind to bear in self-examination. (Which of us is?)

However, he may exercise indirect control over his thoughts and feelings through enlisting the <u>unconscious</u>.

He asks to be beaten. He is spanked. He must deserve it, for he has asked for it. On its conclusion, he is cleansed. Why? Because he paid the forfeit. It's not that he spent fifty minutes

---

2   The subject has, you will note, two outlets for his anger, he can blame the torturer, or himself. But he has undergone the ritual by choice, thus, to his mind, an indictment of the administrator would be fatuous. He is left with "himself."

lying down and talking to some Jew. He's been beaten on the bottom, and every time he tries to sit down, he'll remember that he's paid the price, and now is redeemed, and may go free.

The price for what? IT DOESN'T MATTER.

He's taken a generic beating for an unspecified sin, and everybody's quits. "That's absurd!" the psychoanalysts said. Then I reminded those who had undergone "the treatment" how deuced good they felt on its conclusion, an objection they (in their hearts) could in no wise refute.

Yes, spanking. Or why has it persisted through the ages? (Witness my Middle-Period Ming *chi-hwan*.)

The mention of which brings me to the gist of this reminiscence.

Are there some doors Science was never meant to Open? I am sure of it.

I was involved in some studies in the vicinity of Harvard. A friend at the Kennedy School of Government in Cambridge, Mass threw a cocktail party.

One of the, most interesting, illuminati of that deceptively sedate-looking burg, was an ichthyologist from the Woods Hole Institute.

I mentioned to him my adventures in dry-fly fishing, and he suggested that we repair to my apartment for a cup of tea.

On a hook on the bedroom door, was hung my *chi-hwan*. My friend took it down and enquired after its use. I told him. Returning from some ablutions, I saw him gazing raptly at the thing, his nose a half-inch from the wood.

I was not particularly surprised, as we each had ingested our one-half cc of artificial psilocybin, and were "feeling good."

"What is it, Chet?" I asked.

He raised his head.

"Look at the grain," he said.

I bent my head down and did so.

"Here," he said.

He traced what now appeared plain as day, a vertical pattern in the grain: small parallel lines, now closer together, now farther apart; the lines, each a quarter inch or so, now rising, now falling, now wider apart, now narrowing.

"What do you see?" he said.

"It looks," I said, "like an oscilloscopic rendering of music or speech."

He raised his head and looked at me. "It is the song of the whale," he said.

The next day we took the paddle to the Woods Hole Institute, where it was photographed. The photograph was scanned, and the scan fed into a computer, which interpreted the lines as sound. The sound was played to us. And it, indeed, remarkably resembled the song of a whale. The resemblance far surpassing any reasonable conjecture of "coincidence."

How odd that an elm tree in medieval China would have, hidden in its grain the sound of a whale, you say?

Not odd enough.

For in that "song" I'd heard something.

My friend had not, and when he left the room, I turned the dials to speed up the "whale-like" song, and my suspicions were confirmed. For there, in that room, I heard, in "the song of the whale," a rough but identifiable rendition (though in a Chinese accent) of the words "meet me in Saint Louis."

I destroyed the paddle.

Fate

Wise folks have plumped down on Socrates, or Goethe as the Be-All of Philosophy. Or Emerson, who advocated sitting under trees. (I've read his correspondence with Thoreau, the unexpurgated notes, just released upon the oompth anniversary of his death. And believe you me...)

Well, the Boys like Sitting Under Trees, and God bless 'em. And we're told Socrates just wanted to get out of the house as he was "married to a Yenta." (Yiddish: shrew.)

It all goes into the Pot, and the Pot is the Sum of Human Knowledge. So some put their chips on this fella, and some others on that. Young folk today say "it has no meaning," but they've always said that, until it was time to get a job and/or walk the floor with that colicky kid at four a.m.

I always tell Young Mothers the—one of the few bits of actual practicable knowledge I've acquired: when the colicky kid starts screaming, get up, and go to him, but DON'T LOOK

AT THE CLOCK. There are, of course, wider applications of this principle, and I do not doubt they may occur to you.

A tuna fisherman taught me the only test of knowledge is "would you trust your life to it?" And I'll ride (and indeed have ridden) that horse, until it died under me; and then, walked on, afoot, in gratitude, for the beast's endurance.

But the shining star of philosophy, that, equal to me (and in no wise mutually exclusive of "Kiriea Elesion") ("it's not Just for Easter"), is the verdict on Western Civilization—given in the form of a rhetorical question, by my favorite philosopher: Daffy Duck. For, to poor, unlettered me, the question of life is not that posed by "Dead Thinkers," but, that of a simple duck, who asked, "thaaay, whatthzzzz going on here, anywayyyythzzz...?" Show me the more useful formulation, and I will cleave to it.

I have always believed not only that wisdom is where we find it, but, (this apercu an homage to that Cartoon Character) that the greatest ignorance is the unconsciousness that we are on a quest of knowledge. Yes, not only that knowledge is where we find it, but, if you'll excuse me, that is the only place it is.

For if we don't "find" it, that is, if we don't a) notice it, or b) come across it On Our Own, it is not knowledge. It's, at best, information, and, more usually, cocktail chat. E.G. "Did you see what that (HERE NAME A POLITICIAN OF THE OTHER PARTY) did today?"

I was once the student, and, I believe, the "Muse" of a very wise man. He was, at that time, the head of a consortium of Blind Filipino Masseurs.

And boy did he teach me a thing or two about several things, among them, dealing with disabilities, and occult Oriental practices of you-know-what.

I have before me, on my desk, his gift: a priceless set of Ben Wa balls, fashioned in ivory, the case of ebony inlaid with hieratic figures representative of a cult the identity of which has been lost to time. That's how old they are.

Why have I been spared to live, learn, and collect these reminiscences? I might say it is Part of Some Divine Plan; and I might say that Plan has been facilitated by the knowledge I gained from this Great Masseur—the knowledge not of the Great Scheme of Things, nor of the Human Lot of trial and disappointment (though I learned these, too), but of the location, on the G-5 (spleen) meridian, of a pressure point which enabled me to subdue that troubled youth, run amok in the Stop and Shop in Alexandria, Virginia.

Now you could tell me that this was coincidence: that it was chance that one girl, raised on a farm, but full of sufficient wanderlust to've propelled her into a career in Adult Films—that this girl, in the travels associated with her work, came to become sufficiently skilled in acupressure to subdue a mass murderer before he could cause harm to a store full of Holiday Shoppers.

"What are the odds?" would be one argument for the existence of Fate.

"Ha ha," I am well aware, the purely mathematic-minded would reply. "The odds are ONE HUNDRED PERCENT." How do we know? "BECAUSE IT HAPPENED!"

Alright. I will allow that anything could be, and, in fact, as the physicists would say must, on one level, be coincidence, for it is THE COINCIDENCE OF MOLECULES, or electrons, or whatever the smallest known particle may be this week.

These electrons, (essentially bumper cars, I understand) smash into things creating "light," or "humankind," or whatever they wish. And, according to these Scientists, there is no order beyond this chaos. And "one thing leads to a damned other." According to these chaps, two (or more) electrons "happened" to collide a trillion years ago, creating some interchange which eventually led to Human Kind emerging from the slime mold, the hunter-gatherer civilizations of the Fertile Delta, and, as time went on, literature and the movies.

This "quantum" view of the world must be a lot of fun for folks sitting in cubicles.

I'd respond, "Yes, but so what...? DO YOU WANT TO LIVE IN THAT SORT OF WORLD? Where toast tastes good because of a few electrons eons ago? Or, equally, that's why your daughter married a man who A BLINDMAN could have perceived was NO GOOD?"

I don't know what we got out of this Godless view. As when our accountant loses forty pounds, quits his old firm, marries his yoga teacher, takes our life saving and moves to Peru—even, I assert, the most committed of Godless Academics would (and you know it) curse some Eternal Power who, if delaying evidence of His existence until the financial Tragedy, has deigned to reveal himself at last.

No, no, no, I do not think that this victim would say, "well, it started with the Big Bang, and, so what am I to do?"

If we perceive Order in the World when we are hurt; if we understand ourselves as Chosen when we Win the Lottery, or the fetching young person at the Bar produces a certificate of Sexual health, why are we unprepared to recognize a Divine Plan otherwise?

The Darwinists (and I've known a few) would say we believe in fate because we're just a bunch of stupid apes. But try as I might (and I've spent many an afternoon on the Set, pleasurably debating Chaos versus Divine Intervention), (one of the Big Guns. Others including Free Trade vs. Protectionism, Capitalism vs. a Controlled Economy, Pilates vs. Yoga, and, a perennial favorite, "What is Fashion," which either is or is not odd in a community which spends most of its time stark naked.)

Try as I might, I say, I cannot make sense of an argument which holds that we believe in (what is finally) the Evidence of our Senses, because we are a bunch of stupid monkeys, but: (follow me here) "I," the Darwinist is logically asserting, "have progressed sufficiently beyond that Ape-like Stupidity, that I see THINGS AS THEY REALLY ARE."

But how is this enlightened Darwinist progressed out of the ape-like state, save through the force of a Divine Intelligence or Inspiration. And who would have been in charge of handing this out?

Am I saying, then, that all evolution contrived to place me in the Do It yourself Aisle of the Stop and Shop on that pre-holiday morning?

Yes.

I believe it.

I recall an argument upon the subject with a fan. he was standing outside of the Sound Stage door in Ensenada.

We were shooting ORGY AND BESS, and I was Queen Elizabeth. Taking a cigarette break (in those long-gone Tobacco Days), we'd stepped outside, and there he was. I nodded at him, and he said, "Miss Ranger, I admire your work but take issue with some of your beliefs."

I thought this a poor opening, either for a conversation or a friendship. I was tired (as one always is) from my work on the set, my massive wig was giving me a headache, the corset chafed and my feet were blistered from the Hessian boots. He was a fan, and I've always held it is our responsibility to be courteous to fans.

They can be troublesome, of course; but, as they are human beings and they pay our rent, I've always felt a) be courteous, or b) sneak out the back door.

But we'd been up for hours, trying to salvage a very difficult scene. X, who'd been playing Mary Queen of Scots, had eaten something that morning (God knows what) and couldn't stop barfing.

"Miss Ranger," the fan said, "I must take issue with your views on Fate." I replied to him, "So what?"

Yes, people who've visited The Set, often ask: how do you retain your vim and energy through these endless days: don't you ever get tired? I reply that the life on the set is interesting, and my responsibility to Do My Best and Hold Up Our Side strongly felt. I may or may not tire, but I never feel it til the day is done, and, many times, cannot recall how I managed to get into the car and back to my apartment.

This young fan approached me in that moment between responsibility and surrender, and he, no doubt, found my manner harsh, and undeserved.

I credit myself with some remorse, as I got into the van, charging myself, deservedly, with a breach in manners.

I fell asleep instantly, and did not wake until we stopped, suddenly, at a traffic light outside a shopping center.

"Drive in, Ted," I said, "I want to get some oyster crackers."

This, but for a kind providence, and the long-ago memory of the Blind Masseur, would have been my last words.

For I stepped down from the van, and into the Stop and Shop to buy those essential accoutrements to that bouillabaisse I knew Faustine had waiting for me back Home.

I heard the automatic door open to admit the next customer, then the bark of a rifle, and a man's voice screaming "Oh Yeah…You sons a bitches…!"

Turning, I saw the young fan I had offended, holding a rifle, his satanic rage now, in fact, augmented by the failure of his weapon to "cycle." He was (inexpertly) working the bolt, as I approached him, speaking soft words, my arms open in what began as a Universal Gesture of Peace, and culminated with the application of that pressure on the Spleen Meridian Point which will always induce immediate unconsciousness.

I am glad no one was hurt, and I am contrite in that I spoke "chuff" to him. He was trying to express love, I dismissed him. How that must have hurt. Had I been a whit more courteous, I might have learned from him his views on Fate, and, in fact, found them superior to (as more useful than) my own.

Baseball

Well as My Old Nurse told me... Actually, it was my friend, Patsy Rose Lehrman, the proprietor of the Cozy Time Cabins in which I spent a portion of my "young time on the run."

Patsy referred to herself as The World's Largest Lesbian. And her wisdom was equal to her girth. She'd been, in her time, many things. She read my palm, and told me I would travel to Far Distant Lands. I asked if she could name then, and she said she could—knowledge gained through her service in the Merchant Marine—but that she chose not to.

This, my friend Dieter tells me, is known as Chaos of the Second Level. Chaos, that is, the outcome of which will be affected by predictions.

Dieter taught me that Horse Races are unpredictable. Not only will any given horse on any given day run faster than his or her fellows, but, to cap it off: they're fixed.

So a machine, randomly betting on horse races is participating in Chaos of the First Order. But should some wiseacre or mathematician figure out how to accurately predict the outcome, everyone with that knowledge would run to the window and put it all on the nose of the predicted nag. <u>Then</u>, of course, the price would drop, and, as it dropped, less people would bet on it, making it severely likely, that the "fix" would be put in on <u>another</u> horse. Which one? Dunno. This is Chaos of the <u>Higher</u> Chaos.

Well, I asked him, to what use, then, might a simple country gal put the patsy's prediction?

He was stumped. He told the story all around the Ecole Des Haut Etudes in Paris, and his confreres laughed at what they took, as, either profound, charming naïveté, or more profound wisdom.

They were a skuzzy looking group, I'll tell you that for nothing. Two of them had just escaped being shot, after the War, as Collaborators. They'd joined the Hitler Youth, and, as part of their duties, ratted out their co-Frenchmen who were insufficiently devoted to the Fascists.

I found amusing their sense of superiority. For, though I could not remember how to determine square roots, at least I had not been a sniveling tool of the Huns whose only redeeming feature was the absolute <u>dishiness</u> of their various get-ups.

<u>What</u> a shame, I later told my designers (during that period of my Life in the Rag Biz), that any attempt to max-out, as it were, the B&D look will, inevitably, get tagged as Homage to National Socialism. (Look how they ruined it.)

Pats read my palm and predicted travel, and travel I did. You might say: good looking piece of fluff, run away from home, got to live, and what are the odds she'll settle down and open a dry goods store, or hoe potatoes? Of course she will travel.

But I'd come, as had all the residents, not only of the trailer park, but of the countryside adjoining, to trust Patsy's predictions. If she said it, we would "take it to the bank."

She never charged, nor would she accept gifts, or "payment in kind." She spoke, as any true prophet, from the fullness of her heart. It was a gift, and she shared it fully.

The discerning reader might here comment: Aha, Leafy, have we not just discovered, here and by your own admission, your fall into the trap (just described above) of Second Level Chaos? Perhaps you have travelled, because of your friend's predictions!

Who's to say? Perhaps I have.

And, as to "beware a Tall Dark Stranger," we all (and a young girl especially) should beware of any stranger, you'd say—and you'd not be wrong.

This puts me in mind of a conversation I once had on a long trans-ocean flight, with a representative of UNESCO.

He was off to Niger, bringing with him plans for a water filtration plant. And, dehydrated as we were, on that long-high flight (the cabins, which you may not know, though pressurized, are pressurized only to eight thousand feet). So, after fourteen hours at that height, it's as if you'd been at one-and-a-half times the height of Denver. One of the effects of dehydration (there are many) is the phenomenon, upon exertion, of "a stitch in the side." The muscles or the ligatures or some thing, dehydrated, contract, and there you are.

American Plains Indians, the fellow told me, had a grand method to deal with this. Stand still, they taught their young, find a perfectly round pebble and place it to the side of your right foot. Now bend over <u>laterally</u>, reach down, and pick it up.

See here the practical wisdom.

The young person must, first, stand still, then occupy him or herself looking for the stone (taking the mind off the Trouble). Having done so, the sufferer then puts it by the right foot and reaches down, stretching the intercostal fibers, and rises refreshed.

The man and I spend a two-day layover on Guam, awaiting the arrival of a replacement condenser for the plane's starboard engine.

He invited me to accompany him on his next journey. My schedule did not allow it, and he returned to, and eventually, reestablished amicable relations with his two wives (he was a Doukhobor, originally a Russian sect, migrated to Canada in search of Religious Freedom. Previous generations had practiced castration, then celibacy, but the (then) current doctrine held that we're put here to procreate, or (as I understood it) "there won't be any more Doukhobors," so they (with the benevolent neglect of the Canadian government) engaged in a sort of polygamy, most easily explained as "every other Wednesday."

But who is not charmed (indeed potentially seduced) by Novelty?

"My Old Nurse," then, Patsy Rose, used to let me sit on her porch, and drink her iced tea, and swat flies and talk about life. I say "my Old Nurse," as it is an affectation I picked up from friends in the Special Services Club in London. It is a Britishism. It is outdated, but I like it.

She would say: here it is: keep your eye on the ball, keep your dick in your pants, don't trust nobody but Jesus, and Get the Money Up Front.

I think about her every day.

I hope whatever afterlife she's gone to is agreeable to her.

I hope to meet her there.

Should I do so, I believe she would ask me, "how'd it all work out?" I would respond, "much as you said. Thank you."

We may dream or hear or see a provocative thing. Some of these provoke us to shake our heads, have a drink, or cross the street.

Or we may be moved to re-alter our thinking.

This, I believe, is the purpose of Wisdom. It might also be its definition.

Patsy Rose Lehrman was my first experience of being comforted by wisdom; for, however it unsettles us, if wisdom does not eventually lead to comfort, I think we must call it by another name.

I was very young, and challenged to understand ("first base," "second base," "third base," etc) sexuality.[3] I came to Rose with a story of an encounter, and she chuckled. I was hurt, and asked her, "What's so funny?" And she answered, "Sex."

"Sex," I said, "Sex is funny...?"

"You don't think it's funny," she said, "watch two people doing it."

Well, I took her up on it, and spent many an afternoon, peeping through knotholes at the Cozy Time Cabins.

That, believe me, was an education.

I saw and heard things which provoked me. I might say, that those afternoons were like the musings of the Wright Brothers. They'd been told one thing: Man Can Not Fly; but they lazed around, on their backs, watching birds.

Well, then, they thought, what debarred <u>man</u> from flight? What did they conclude? His <u>consciousness</u>.

Knowing that flight was possible, others were stunted by the <u>notion</u> that Man could not fly. It was not that birds were better equipped physically (though, of course, they were), but that they were not crippled by false notions.

---

3   This, I explained, years later, in the locker room of (a Major League Team, with whom I was doing some Charity Work), was my first exposure to the intricacies not only of sex, but of baseball. On hearing my confession they began to hoot with laughter, give each other "high-fives," hop around and clap one another on the back. I had, decades before, seen a near-identical display on Bora Bora: it was the Pantomime of the Double Outrigger. How to account for the similarity? I cannot, save to suggest that all human behavior is, like sex, limited in variety: there are "only so many ways you can do it."

It was here, in considering Rose's *bon mot*, in the light of my laboratory observations, that I came to a better understanding. All that writhing around on the cot was funny because it was sad.

Why was it sad? Because the folks involved were human beings doomed to desire and die. Watching those people, in that light, was the least aphrodisiacal experience of my life.

Later I saw my first adult film. Now why, I wondered, is this (at least in potential) fulfilling, while the less structured puts one off?

I put the question, over the years, not only to psychiatrists, but to film makers, and oculists. Each you may be sure, had his own response, bringing his own expertise (and, so, prejudices) to bear. One was adept at this and one at that, BUT NONE AT PORNOGRAPHY.

I realized, then, that the answer to the question rested with me. Because I spent those hours at the knothole, driven not by my desires for gratification, but in the search for knowledge, I was, you might say saddled, (I would say rewarded), with a calling.

Do you scoff?

When I, as related, first saw my friend Delores, far far from the Convent, clothed only in the eel-skin G-string, my first thought was "you whore. You told me you would never wear garments of animal skin. Where is your Vegetarianism Now?"

But she explained to me, she wore it in service to the Wishes of her Tribe.

That's why I made pornographic films.

Priscilla Wriston-Ranger
Montreux, Switzerland
June 2018

Author's Biography

Priscilla Wriston-Ranger (Pamela Kotz) was born and raised in Central Michigan. After a brief stint in the U.S. Forest Service, she embarked upon that career in Adult Entertainment which would span three decades, and all continents. Her travels, as actress, writer, director, and Personal Consultant, sparked those interests and friendships which persist, to this day, in her philanthropic work. She lives in Montreux, Switzerland.

R.

Tart with a Heart

An Afterword by David Mamet

Freud wrote that examining the "song stuck in one's head" one might discover something of the workings of one's consciousness.

I found myself humming "Frivolous Sal," a song was written in 1905 by Paul Dresser. *"They call her frivolous Sal / A peculiar sort of gal."* It was an ode to his lover, who was the madam of a brothel in Terre Haute, Indiana.

Dresser is best known today for his "On the Banks of the Wabash, Far Away" (1897), but in his own day cherished both "Sal" and the even more popular "Just Tell Them That You Saw Me."

This last is the report of a country boy, come to the big city, who discovers on the pavement an old school chum, now a streetwalker. "Just tell them that you saw me," she said, "they'll know the rest." At the turn of the twentieth century, Dresser was known as the King of Broadway, and "just tell them that you saw me" was a catchphrase of the turn-of-the-century period.

His brother was the great novelist Theodore Dreiser.

My favorite of Dreiser's books, unfortunately little read today and eclipsed in academic note by *Sister Carrie*, was *Jennie Gerhardt*, the story of a prostitute who becomes the devoted mistress of a wealthy Chicagoan.

Dreiser also took up the theme in *The Stoic* (1947), the final volume of the *Trilogy of Desire*. Here, Frank Cowperwood (Charles Yerkes), a phenomenally wealthy financier, falls in love with the photograph of a child.

The photo is in the boudoir of a friend of his, a madam. It is the photo of her teenage daughter. Cowperwood searches out the girl, becomes her protector, and, eventually, persuades her to become his mistress, a position she occupies, with devotion, until his death. (See also Marion Davies, mistress of W. R. Hearst, who, on his fall to financial ruin, hocked her jewels for him.)

I began musing on the subject of the Tart with a Heart, and, as after the first revelation of Fibonacci numbers or Official Corruption, once sensitized, perceived it everywhere.

The book of Joshua contains the story of Rahab the Harlot. It was she who aided the Israelites in their conquest of Jericho. I am unacquainted with previous instances of the character, but perhaps they will occur to the reader.

But consider the modern instances, which a lack of application will induce me to supply in no particular order. Consider *Roxana: The Fortunate Mistress* (Daniel Defoe, 1724) and his *Moll Flanders* (1722), perhaps the first "modern" reiterations of the story.

Also, Thomas De Quincey's platonic love of the prostitute in *Confessions of an English Opium-Eater* (1821); the staid George Eliot's *Romola* (1863); John Cleland's *Fanny Hill: Memoirs of a Woman of Pleasure* (1748). Crossing the Channel, we find perhaps the most iconic example in Alexander Dumas fils's *La Dame aux Camélias* (1848), the story of the openhearted courtesan Marguerite, who gives her life for her young lover. The novel has been adapted to the stage more than twenty times, provides the libretto for *La traviata*, and was filmed twice, including as the 1936 Greta Garbo classic *Camille*.

Moving from romance to realism, we find Émile Zola's career of a whore in *Nana* (1880), and, continuing, much of the work of Colette (1873–1954). If the sign of a cultural phenomenon is the translation from one medium to another, consider Colette's 1944 novel *Gigi*, about a young girl raised to be a courtesan, and transmogrified by Vincente Minnelli et al. into a romantic musical screen fantasy.

Consider the works of Guy de Maupassant. His novellas *Boule de Suif* (1880) and *Madame Tellier's Establishment* (1881) are pristine and magnificent examples of the genre—the first, the tale of a whore, and the second, of a whorehouse—and vastly influential in their influence on English literature and films.

Note Somerset Maugham's masterpiece *Of Human Bondage*, a novel about the hero's tragic love of a streetwalker, and his short story *Rain*.

Maugham (who spoke French before he spoke English) was the direct artistic descendant of Maupassant, dealing extensively with prostitution and adultery. In *Rain*, a fallen woman washes up on a tropical isle and leads a missionary to ruin.[4] These hard-hearted women, along with *The Blue Angel*, seem signal outliers in the Prostitution genre, the majority of which are, as in Maupassant, *the whore with a heart of gold*.

Boule de Suif (*Butterball*) is the story of upright burghers and their wives, trapped in a coach with a common whore. She feeds them, amuses them, and, eventually, sacrifices herself for them, giving herself to a vile Prussian officer who is holding the coach captive until she acquiesces. This story was made famous in America in the films *Stagecoach* (1939), in which the whore is played by Claire Trevor; in *Shanghai Express* (1932, Anna May Wong); and may be found also in the Garbo film *Conquest* (1937). Here, she is a Polish aristocrat, who must give herself to Napoleon in order to draw his attention to the plight of Poland.

See also *That Hamilton Woman,* about the good-heartedness of Emma Hamilton, ex-prostitute, whose love salves

---

4   With additional material previously unpublished, and emendations based on my interviews with the author.

the heart of Admiral Nelson, and the absolutely sure-fire tear-jerker *Waterloo Bridge*. Robert Sherwood's 1930 play about a nice girl reduced to the streets was transferred (very successfully) to the screen in 1931, with Mae Clarke in the lead, and again in 1940, with Vivien Leigh.

The story is also recast as the FBI Against the Nazis in Alfred Hitchcock's *Notorious* (1946). Here, Cary Grant convinces Ingrid Bergman to marry the vile ex-Nazi Claude Rains in order to obtain information.

In contemporary literature we find the Tart with a Heart in *A House Is Not a Home* (1953) by Polly Adler, a Washington, D.C., madam, and its derivative, *The Happy Hooker* (1971) by Xaviera Hollander. Popular modern instances include *Sarah* (1980) by JT LeRoy, a novel about a tender-hearted young male hustler; Scotty Bowers's *Full Service* (2012), the memoir of a Hollywood stud-hustler and pimp; and, most famously, *Breakfast at Tiffany's* (1961).

The contemporary film *Red Sparrow* (2018) is full of (simulated?) sex and a lot of gore, but there it is in the framework of the thing: the injured ballerina, no longer able to dance, must go to Russian spy/prostitute school in order to obtain medical care for her mom. At the film's end, she, of course, winds up betraying her masters in order to serve her new love, the American spy: the Tart with a Heart.

It is clear we the cherish the myth. And why not? It allows us to enjoy the titillating in full assurance that it will, eventually, lead to a revelation of virtue. An old and useful dodge:

*Throughout the infinite variety of this Book, this funda-
mental is most strictly adhered to; there is not a wicked
Action in any Part of it but is first or last rendered
Unhappy and Unfortunate. There is not a superlative
villain brought upon the stage, but either he is brought to
an unhappy end, or brought to be a Penitent.*

—DANIEL DEFOE, *Moll Flanders* (1722)

My musings took me to the bookshelf, to the (privately printed) *One Woman's Quest*, here reissued[5] as *The Diary of a Porn Star.*

I hope I may be forgiven for a somewhat academic approach in this essay to that which a reader may have obtained in a legitimate quest for the salacious; and I applaud Ms. Ranger (as she does both Bettie Page and Gypsy Rose Lee) for the largely successful, and quite enjoyable, attempt to regularize our natural human voyeurism, cleansing the product and, thus, the reader of shame for the most natural of interests.

David Mamet
August 2019

---

5   With additional material previously unpublished, and emendations based on my
     interviews with the author.